The Green Hotel

The Green Hotel

Jesse Gilmour

QUATTRO BOOKS

The publication of *The Green Hotel* has been generously supported by the Canada Council for the Arts and the Ontario Arts Council.

 Canada Council   Conseil des Arts
for the Arts   du Canada

 ONTARIO ARTS COUNCIL
CONSEIL DES ARTS DE L'ONTARIO

an Ontario government agency
un organisme du gouvernement de l'Ontario

Cover design: Sarah Beaudin
Author photo: Curtis Stewart
Editor: Luciano Iacobelli
Typography: Natasha Shaikh

Library and Archives Canada Cataloguing in Publication

Gilmour, Jesse, author
          The green hotel / Jesse Gilmour.

ISBN 978-1-927443-70-5 (pbk.)

          I. Title.

PS8613.I529G74 2014   C813'.6   C2014-905781-4

Published by Quattro Books Inc.
Toronto
www.quattrobooks.ca

Printed in Canada

Before I formed you in the womb I knew you.

– Jeremiah 1:5

For Maurice Farge

I dreamt that night that I was standing on the cliffs behind the green hotel, the ones that lead into the ocean. He's fifty feet below me in the black.

"What happened, Dad?"

He yells to make sure I can hear him from the water.

"Someone burned it down, son!"

I watch him swim for a while. He's treading water, going in a circular motion. He doesn't seem concerned that the water is cold. I ask him if I should come down. He tells me not to worry, he'll come up. He starts to swim towards the bottom of the cliff; he pauses for a second and then starts to climb. The ascent is absolutely flat but he seems to manage. All I can hear are the crickets and the gushing of the waves. He is silent on the rocks. There is something odd about him – I can't put my finger on it until he's about six feet out.

It's his hair. It is slicked across his back like some kind of armour. It stretches delicately past his feet and stays submerged as he climbs. He tells me he'll be there soon.

"What burned down, Dad?"

I turn around to look at the green hotel – there is a beautiful woman in a plastic party hat smoking a cigarette by the dusty patio chairs. She doesn't ask why I'm out there, who I'm waiting for, what I'm doing, she minds her business. I have a private hope that she'll go inside before he arrives.

When he does arrive, when his face pops up in front of the cliff's edge and his hair, miles of it, flickers in the night behind him and stretches taut to the very bottom of the ocean, he puts his hand on my face.

Two P.M.

Both of us want to live underwater.

I open my eyes fully to see the June light stagger through my window and plonk itself down onto the green comforter above my right shin. It's two o'clock in the afternoon. For a long time my father woke me up in the morning, but he doesn't anymore.

I go through the motions of waking up as if I'm being watched: the stretching, the empty yawning.

I can hear him walking from the kitchen to the living room and back again – over and over.

I've left a hammer on the wooden floor. I step on it as I get out of bed. I sit down when that happens. I watch my foot bleed for a minute or so and then put a black sock over it and light a cigarette. I look out the window; there are, as usual, a lot of Asians out there today.

I open my door and walk softly into the hallway. The walls are lined with paintings of me, five of them to be exact, five paintings leading to the sixth in his study. I don't bother opening the door quietly. He knows I'm awake now.

It looks less ominous this morning, less like a stamp of ruin. Of the six, it is the only one where you can't see my face. It is the painting that landed me in jail. I stare at it, bleary-eyed, waking up still.

When I turn around he's beside me.

He's short, my Dad, 5'6" maybe, he has a grey buzz cut and a grey beard. He's wearing a black t-shirt and purple basketball shorts. He's unshaven. He's sensitive looking, as though the gears controlling his insides haven't been oiled and are just a bit too close to the skin; their movement causes small vibrations on his face that you can almost see if you look close enough.

"You still hate it?" he asks me.

I put my arm out and drape it across his shoulder. I look at him, and then back at the easel.

"Yeah, but that's alright, let's have breakfast anyway."

We live in a two-floor loft a block away from Chinatown, but you can see it from the window in my room. In the day it's depressing, figures moving too quickly, selling garbage. They strike me as the kind of people who wouldn't help you even if you really needed it.

At night it's pretty, though. It's a mysterious place and even before we moved to the area I'd go there as a teenager, always at night, just to walk around and watch the people in the corridors of gambling halls and in the windows of the orange-lit restaurants. There were alleyways in Chinatown that seemed like they'd been there for hundreds of years. I'd sit in them alone and smoke cigarettes, and later on, I'd go there to drink.

On the corner of the street, before Chinatown *happens*, there is an abandoned house. It has been there since the beginning and in the dark you can see the edge of a neon yellow sign peeking over the roof.

We head downstairs to the kitchen together. My bail papers are on the table. He sits down and looks at them and smiles.

"You want to make breakfast or should I?" he asks.

"I'll make it," I say.

"Slow and low, with the eggs, you know that, right?"

"Yeah, I know."

He puts my bail papers aside and looks out the window.

I come around the table and stand behind him and put my hands on the back of his neck.

"You all good, Dad?"

"I'm good, I'm good," he says and puts his hand on one of mine. His shoulders are sweaty through his t-shirt.

I hear him pick the bail papers up again while I'm cracking the eggs into the pan.

"What does 'release on your recognizance' mean?'"

"I wasn't released on my own recognizance, Dad."

"No, I know, but I heard it once and I've always been curious about it."

I turn the heat down and whisk the eggs together.

"It's when they let you go with no bail."

"Oh," he says.

When breakfast is finished he tells me that he'd like to start drinking.

"Let's move into the living room, though. I'd like to sit in the living room and have a drink and talk. You know – this Armenian illustrator that was an influence of mine, in his biography it said that every night around now, around five o'clock, when the sun was going down like this, he'd start to get sad…"

There was no point in telling me that the guy was Armenian, but my Dad was smart like that – he'd add little details to make things clear.

"…his wife knew this, and so she'd light candles and put on some music and they'd have drinks. That's what I'd like to do…let's move into the living room."

03

The first time I noticed something was wrong with him was on Father's Day when I was nine. I'd heard the kids at school talking about it but didn't pay much attention. Perhaps the fact that my mother wasn't around made me feel kind of exempt from it, I don't know.

Anyways, it was a Saturday morning and I was sleeping late in the blue room that overlooked the park and the dogs in it. We lived in a different apartment when I was young, a smaller one – this is long before he sold any paintings and he still cut down trees for a living.

When I looked up he was standing there, his hair in a ponytail. He was angry, yes, but there was a look in his face that seemed sad, too. As if he'd tried, all morning, to not come in – but just kept thinking about it and thinking about it until it broke him. Underneath the rage, he looked resigned.

"Where's my fucking present, Hayden?"

He gritted his teeth and said it again, this time he yelled.

"Where is my fucking present?"

I knew now that he wasn't joking, and I sat straight up in my bed and stared at him.

He told me that he did a lot for me, that I was ungrateful, that he was sick of this – all of it.

He smashed the white door with his hand a couple of times and then he left.

I got up after a while and cleaned the kitchen. I did the dishes, sprayed the cabinets with Windex, and wiped them with paper towel. I went to the back where the laundry room was and started to get the mop out of the mop bucket when I heard him come back up. I stayed in the room for a second, looking at the dark purple mop bucket and the dry, spindly white mop sticking out of it.

He said my name and then sat down at the marked wooden table in the living room. He said he was sorry. I told him I'd done the kitchen. He thanked me and then we went out for breakfast.

Ↄ

He sits in the beige armchair by the window and puts a glass between his thighs. I watch him pour his drink. Even with the glass unsteady like that he pours it precisely – he's an exact kind of guy. The things he likes – art, booze, music – he treats with respect.

"You know what, Dad – I will have one."

He puts the glass down and goes into the kitchen and comes back with a glass for me.

"You like drinking in the day?" he asks me.

"Yeah, of course,"

"What do you like about it?"

I haven't had a drink in a couple of months – you start up with dope and quickly realize how *facile* alcohol is.

"For the first couple you feel very…optimistic about your day. The moments of the day, the ones ahead of you, just kind of blur together and everything is just…soft and…"

"Promising?"

"Yeah, promising – but only for the first couple…then you just feel like shit. That's why I like *what I like*."

He takes a sip and nods.

"Well, feel free to do that whenever you want. The role-model ship has sailed, has it not?"

He drains his glass and puts it back between his thighs. I get up and stand at the window behind him. For years, while in the same room with him, I felt nervous about moving around. He didn't like the distraction of movement while talking.

It is freeing, I have to say, to get up and go to the window like that.

You know in Hiroshima when the shadows were burned into the ground? That's how the sky looks while the sun is going down, like someone has set fire to the village up there, changing the colour of the landscape forever – everything pastels now, old horror turning pretty after a thousand years.

I wonder, for a second, if it's bothering him that I'm standing here. Or has he let go? Is he thinking about other things? It's strange, that, just the thought that he would have anything else to think about but me.

He clears his throat. That's enough, I think. I turn around and put my hands back on his shoulders.

He stiffens up when I do it.

"Why do you keep touching me like that?"

"Like what?"

"It's troubling, the way you touch me. Sorry, I don't mean to be difficult."

"You're not being difficult."

I take my hands off his shoulders and sit back down across from him. He pours himself another drink, precisely, like before.

"You want another one?"

"Sure. …Do you mind if I make a suggestion, Dad?"

"Of course not."

"You should change into something nicer…"

He pauses and takes another sip of vodka.

"You're right – it embarrassed me when you first said it, just now when you first said it…but you're absolutely right. I'm going to…will you tell me a story about jail first, though? I've always been curious about jail. I think most men are…I think most men wonder how they would *fare.*"

"I got thrown on a shitty range," I say. "I don't think the admissions cop liked me…"

"Everyone likes you, Hayden."

And mostly they did, he was right, but it was obvious that the admissions officer didn't because he threw me onto a range with all blacks. Range C. They called it, unfortunately, "The Jungle Range."

Usually when white guys get thrown into the Don for bullshit offences like mine they get offered protective custody – this is pretty humiliating. I mean, Damon wouldn't have let me live it down if I'd gone in there: it's generally for rats and people who fuck around with kids and those who can't handle themselves, so I was kind of flattered that he never even offered it. It meant he saw some strength in me, prick that he was.

"More than anything, Dad, it's boring. There's no women there, right? So it's a dead place. A dead zone…man, it's fucking boring…"

My phone goes off, it's Damon, but I don't pick it up.

"Is that Damon?"

"Yeah, I'll call him back."

"Are you sure you don't want to get it?"

"I already talked to him, don't worry."

"Okay…you know what you're doing…"

He drains his vodka and puts his feet up on the coffee table.

I repeat, "There are no women there, right? So, it's…a dead place. A dead zone. It's a dead zone…there's a trick to it, though. You want to know the trick?"

He takes a belt.

"What's the trick?"

"You must be yourself – you laugh when you find something funny, and don't when you don't – never laugh *at* anyone. No putting on that special walk that you think makes you look cool. You walk to move…you laugh when you find something funny, you eat when you're hungry, you talk to express something you need to express, you listen when you *need* to listen. You bring it right back down to the basics *and that way no one can smell anything fake on you.* Self-consciousness will get you humiliated. There was one kid, they made him walk around the range with underwear on his head, naked. And he was pretending it was funny, that it was all a joke…man, that's the most fucked up thing I've ever seen in my life. Not the underwear on his head, but the way he pretended it was all good…all fun…"

My phone goes off a second time. It's Damon again, this time a text message.

I can't come through until like one or some shit how many do you want?

I ask him how many he wants. He tells me thirty-four. I tell him he doesn't need thirty-four. He says he wants thirty-four anyway. I text Damon the numbers thirty-four. Damon texts back *fuck* immediately and then *okay.*

"Why thirty-four, Dad?"

He pours a half ounce of vodka into his glass and rubs the side of his face.

"That's how old Christ was when he died…"

I pause and look at him.

"A little *grand*, I know…but that's how many I want. Besides – we might as well overdo it…I don't want to wake up in a cold bathtub with a hangover…you know what I mean, Hayden?"

"Yeah," I say.

"Just make sure it's thirty-four…I'm going to have a little nap, if that's alright with you… thanks for the jail story…"

He gets up rapidly, opens his eyes wide, smiles at me, and walks to the bottom of the stairs. He turns around before he goes.

"What time is he coming?"

"One."

"Okay, then."

When he's gone I lie on the couch, it smells like him. The room feels very empty without him. I consider that for a second.

Samantha's shoes, her blue and white Converse, have been in my closet for three years. She left them here on the last day we saw each other. The shoes scare me, to be honest. Until today, I've always been afraid to touch them.

When I open the closet, there they are still, lifeless. I pick them up by the tongues and put them in the corner where the walls meet and get the pill and the syringe and the cooker out of my front jacket pocket. I unscrew the pill carefully, keeping in mind the way he poured the vodka. I dump the beads onto my desk and take a piece of paper, a cell phone bill, and lay it over them. You have to do this or they'll scatter when you smash them with a hammer – which I do next. When I peel up the paper there's a thick yellowish powder underneath which I scrape gently into the small cooker that I got from the walk-in clinic. I take a fresh syringe, pop off the blue cap, and suck some water from a glass on my nightstand. I fire the water into the cooker, put the lighter under until it bubbles, add some more water – I do this three times.

Hydromorph-Contin has to be cooked three times.

I take the blue plastic tie and wrap it around my wrist. I hit the vein in my hand; it flags after the third shot and a thin strand of blood shoots in the barrel.

I press down slowly.

The rush is so good it makes my eyes water – exploding pins and needles, starting in the knees, to the chest, to the neck, and finally the feet.

I look over at Samantha's shoes.

Then I start to nod.

ভ

When I was fifteen years old, my father stayed in his room for two weeks. One afternoon, he came into the kitchen stark naked and said, simply, "I've got a problem, Hayden." He put his pajamas on and we took a taxi down to the Queen Street CAMH. He made jokes in the cab, funny observations about people on the street, and by the time we got to the brown brick building I was laughing. After a quick conversation with a chubby, red-haired doctor, he was admitted to the psychiatric ward on the ninth floor. I told the doctor I was going to stay with my mother for a while – this was something we'd discussed on the ride over.

I walked home through the blue grey, and when I got there a couple of hours later I took some CDs out of my drawer and went into his room and laid them out on his bed. He hung all his clothes on pine hangers and so his room always smelled fresh. I got up and looked in his closet; twelve black t-shirts, hanging, twelve dads.

Damon came over that night around one; he'd just broken into a house on Dupont and had three hundred dollars in loonies and toonies jammed in his khaki short pockets. He did a little dance before he scattered them across our dining room table. He asked me that night, gazing up at the paintings of sharks and porches, the beginnings of red stubble starting to appear on his face, if my father had ever painted me. I told him no. When he asked why, I responded as Damon responded to everyone except me, monosyllabically, and without detail.

The truth was I didn't know why I never let him. I just felt that there was something *off* about it.

We spent the week smoking hash, trying to get girls over, and ordering the kind of take-out you order when you're fifteen and have more money than you're supposed to.

They released him on Father's Day. We went out for hamburgers and when he asked me this time if he could paint me, his eyes small and frightened, his voice shaky, I obliged. To be honest, I felt that I owed him.

His study smelled like wax and the moon outside looked like it had been amputated from something vaster.

I closed my eyes while his arm moved. He told me not to close my eyes.

It didn't take that long, it was more of a sketch than a painting. When the fifteen minutes were up he seemed to brighten. I got out of the red chair and went around the easel to look at what he'd done. I liked the way I looked, I looked handsome.

I told him he could do it more if he wanted.

He gave me twenty dollars for pizza and then went out for dinner by himself, the hospital band still on his wrist.

Later on, as I sat in the living room and tried to watch television, it came over me, just like that, that I never wanted to see him again. At first I batted it away as perversity, like jumping in front of a subway train or grabbing an old woman's purse. There was a sharpness to the thought, though, a clarity to it that seemed terrifying and otherworldly, but above all, *correct*.

As if I was watching myself sleepwalk, I turned off the television and without locking up behind me stepped into the summer night. Someone had spray-painted a yellow line across the door of the abandoned house.

This was years, and years, and years before I tried to burn it down.

I walked to Chinatown and got on the streetcar. I paid my fare and slumped myself into one of the back seats and closed my eyes until I could feel the vibrations of the tracks shift.

I got on the northbound train because I'd never been uptown before. I'd heard from Damon that "beautiful, rich sluts" lived there so that might have had something do with it – but it was more about going somewhere new. I got into a stare-down with a sullen black kid on the train. Staring at someone past the point where it's uncomfortable is a muscle you develop growing up in Toronto. At first it seems so foreign, laughable and scary at the same time – but it gets easier.

He got off at St. Clair. I waved to him through the drifting windows as the train pulled away. He frowned at me.

I ducked into a Korean convenience store outside of Eglinton Station and walked east until I hit Grayson. The streets were wider than in Chinatown, and there was a sexy calmness to them that I've associated with rich girls, and the lighting in their bedrooms, ever since. It was more than comfort, though. There was something death-like about it, a little *too cozy*. Too good.

I was looking for a park, for empty green sprawl. I could picture it in my head, I wanted to hear water move, to see the brown, smudge-like silhouettes of wolves through the fog. That was where I was going to make my mark, where I was going to reverse things.

I walked until I came to one. I stepped off the concrete and onto the grass and looked down. It was so vast I could imagine it reaching all the way back to my father's bedroom. You would just have to take the right path. The crickets sounded different out there. I think that's because the things in my neighbourhood weren't crickets, they were something else. He told me the name of them once.

I noticed three guys in fitted hats and bad skin drinking on a bench at the entrance of the ravine. They were not from Yonge and Eglinton, but hey, neither was I.

They looked over and stared. Their hats had no team symbols on them, they were plain black. They were bored, and drunk, and in a neighbourhood where the women would always be unattainable to them – and so I knew there was a pretty good chance they were going to hurt me.

Not before I light my fire, though, I thought. They'll have to kill me, I thought.

I scanned the words in my head to see if I was bullshitting. I wasn't.

One of them raised his forty up in the air in salute. I nodded and made my way into the ravine.

I walked until I could hear water, until, like a spear sticking out of the ground, I saw a wooden sign. It said something like "more park that way" and had an arrow. I could hear my three pals from the top of the ravine, their voices blending in with the moving cars. I took the lighter fluid out of the plastic bag and covered the sign in it. Like really fucking covered it. I used half the bottle. I lit the box of wooden matches with my lighter, and placed it at the base.

I watched it go…the dark red and dark purple…reaching around the sign, the flames chasing each other.

I liked the feeling on my face and the way my shadow looked beneath the fire.

I noticed, while the thing burned, that my thoughts seemed to kind of *consolidate*. Everything had a perfect mathematical equation to it: there was a beginning, a middle and an end to everything.

The end was a nicely rounded conclusion…and then on to the next thought. There was no grasping at anything, no fear, no shrieking at the edges. I felt unaware of my brain, or my arms, or my penis. It was as if I'd made a little friend off in the distance who waved at me from miles and miles away.

Forty-five seconds.

Fifty-five seconds.

When the hundred seconds were up I made my way back up the path.

When I got to the top I asked them if I could buy a beer, they said five dollars. I walked back onto Grayson Street drinking the warm liquid, walking slowly, imagining the park burning and the three boys watching it.

I felt, for the first time in my life, like I'd accomplished something. Like life had tried to make a move on me, but I had made a move on it.

At the end of Grayson Street, before I got to the main intersection that led to the subway, I saw her.

She was blonde with a pink mouth. She was wearing shorts and she had just returned from a trip. She sat on the back fender while her parents lugged shit up to the front door – steep stairs reaching up the green hill that all the houses on the block rested on: dignified, relaxed.

There were only two things that I desired more than the girl herself, with her back slouched against the trunk of the car and her flip-flops on the ashy, moonlit concrete of her driveway: where she was going, and where she had come from. We wouldn't meet again for years, but that was the first time I saw Samantha.

SIX P.M.

As I make the way down the stairs I can hear soft blues music coming from the vintage speakers next to his bookcases. He's put the Christmas lights up; blue and red and purple and gold blinking away, perfectly symmetrical except for a small dip like a noose at the top.

He's changed, he's wearing dark jeans, a red t-shirt and an expensive black blazer. He has his legs crossed so I can see his purple Polo socks with the little horse. There is a prescription bottle of Valium on the coffee table, lit up by a beeswax candle, and next to that a bottle of Stolichnaya.

"I like those candles," I say.

"You know it cleans the air? Did you know that?"

"Yeah, I think you told me that before."

On his lap is a book on the Basque Conflict. He reads about war, mostly.

"You know what I was thinking about just now?"

I shake my head.

"I was thinking that when you were little, like nine or ten, I could have left you anywhere...I could have left you in Spain and you would have been okay. I don't know why I was thinking about that, but I was. Are you hungry? You want a hamburger?"

I shake my head and pick up the bottle of Stolichnaya. I want to feel how cold it is.

"I remember when you used to keep it in the snow," I say.

And I do remember, him coming up the porch stairs in his blue puff coat, holding the bottle of freezing vodka, his hands wet. We drank until five o'clock in the morning that night – it was a year or so after Samantha had left. He said, before he wobbled upstairs to bed, "She's coming back, you know...like a grey ship...and you're the only one waiting at the port..."

She never came back. He was wrong.

He tells me that Mason is arriving in twenty minutes. They're going out for dinner. He asks me if that's okay. I say yes, of course it's okay.

Next to the bookcase, over his shoulder, is the first sketch of the first painting Mason sold for him. The finished product was a lot more detailed, but both were of Lantern Sharks.

Lantern Sharks are the smallest sharks on the planet – they're about a foot long. You can find them in the Icelandic waters, and near South Africa, too. I was sixteen years old when he sold it. He was cutting down trees on Mason's property up north near Muskoka and when he went into the house to hand over the invoice he saw the art on the walls. He told Mason that he painted, and that he was very good.

He was. Mason sold the shark painting for him within a month. My Dad got down on his knees when he found out. I remember him, down on his knees, thanking God when it happened. When the cheque came through he gave me five thousand dollars with a note attached that read:

With admiration, respect and a firm knowing that you are a better person than me.

He was good for a couple of months after that. Only a couple, though – he told me once, a little while later, that it had made things worse.

"Now that I am successful I dislike *people* more. Before, I only disliked myself. There is something about success that makes you *angry* with people."

The paintings kept selling, though. One after another until he was in the newspaper and all kinds of women started coming around. He'd always been good with women, but these ones were different – they were young, they felt closer to my age than his. He'd talk about me a lot in front of them, how good looking I was, how smart I was. It felt, sometimes, like he was trying to set them up with me.

I was proud of him. He'd done it. It didn't make a difference to how he felt in his day, but I always had a suspicion
that it was important he'd gotten some recognition. It was
important at the edges of things.

When the doorbell rings I let Mason in. It's been six
months since we've seen each other and he looks old. He's
approaching eighty and walks with a cane. He has a serene
face, thick eyebrows and floppy white hair. He's wearing
cheap, immaculate black running shoes with Velcro straps
and a blue and white striped shirt with sailboats on it.
He grins when he sees me, he's always liked me. He even
came to my high school graduation. It was like having my
grandfather in the crowd.

He puts his hand on my shoulder and says, "Klara told
me to say hello to you…"

I'd dated his daughter about a year back, only briefly, and
before the opiates had completely catapulted my sex drive.
I exited pretty gracefully but I've always felt bad about it.
I've been nervous about seeing him, to be honest – worried
he's been mad at me. But he's too wise for that, I think – too
wise to be mad at people.

My father stands up and puts his arm out. He says, "My
boss…and my boy! What a night, what a great fucking
night…isn't that something?"

Mason ambles in and sets his cane against the couch.
He hugs my father. One of the Christmas lights has
inexplicably gone out.

"There are so many beautiful women out there tonight,"
he says. "Toronto has the most beautiful women in the
world, I think. It must…"

Of the two or three scraps we'd had, the worst was the
night he turned on Mason.

My father's real dark spells, the ones that would have
him in his room for a couple of weeks, or wandering around
in the housing projects three blocks away trying to score
downers, were always preceded by a purge of negativity.

He'd start in about how talentless other painters in Toronto were, or how ludicrous it was that the hippies in the park were looked at by the community as harmless when in reality they were junkie scum who "probably pimp out their girlfriends."

Generally I'd agree with him, and he'd be funny about it, and before I knew *where it all wound up* I never looked at his rants as a bad thing.

One night I came home and he told me he was firing "that fucking vampire Mason."

A deal had fallen through and apparently it hadn't been broken to my father with enough compassion, or respect, or whatever. We got in an argument about it – an argument that ended with a black eye for him and a broken pinky finger for me. At the time I rationalized my anger about it as outrage for his callousness. Mason had, after all, made my Dad a lot of money, made him a real painter. And he'd let the toxicity in him turn on the one little bright patch in his life.

Maybe I was angry at the fact that his success hadn't really changed anything, I don't know…

Maybe I worried that if he could turn on Mason the spotlight could fall on me next.

Maybe it was many different things, things I couldn't even really grasp at the time – the kitchen sink overflowing because the one in the basement is blocked.

There's a certain mythology about fighting your Dad, and although I think everyone should punch their father in the face at least once in their life, it didn't change anything – it just made me feel terrible – and I was still scared of him, in my special way, afterwards.

"That's why Australians come here," I say. "For the women…"

Mason nods and laughs.

"I've never liked Australian men," Mason says.

"Me neither," I say.

I pour myself a drink and watch the lights behind him. They seem to shriek a little bit. I think about how soft they'll be once I do another shot. That, right there, is why it's so hard to get away from the stuff.

Observations like that.

"Behind every man's self-lacerating fantasy of their wife's infidelity is an Australian man. Even if they're not Australian…they're Australian," my Dad says.

"They're shadow people," I say. "They have no eyes."

"Australians?"

"No," I say. "The guys you think are fucking your girlfriend…or your ex-girlfriend…or whatever. They have no eyes. Try at some point to think about their eyes – you can't. Try to *actually* picture them – you can't. They are made of shadow."

"But terrifying, nonetheless," Mason says.

My father looks over at me and nods softly. He has always said there is something about Mason that brings out the best in me.

I watch them talk for the next half an hour. Only I know this, but my father has no curiosity about anything anymore. He did when I was little – he'd talk to cab drivers and E.R. nurses and Filipino nannies on the streetcar – he'd ask questions about their lives with genuine interest and you could see their faces brighten when he did. And even though the actual core is gone now, the shell of the curiosity still exists – and the shell is good enough to make people like you in this world. A lot of people would give everything for just the shell. He asks Mason about his wife, about his *other* daughter in law school. He is interested and self-effacing and makes articulate and well-seasoned observations about things. It is only I who can hear the rusty clank of machinery in the darkened warehouse.

Mason takes a sip and looks over at me. He's a little tuned up from the vodka. He says, "You look like my brother…did

I ever tell you that? His hair was lighter than yours, but he was still blond like you."

"Spent his entire twenties in jail," my Dad says. "Ten. Fucking. Years. Did I never tell you that, Hayden?"

"No," I say. He has, but I want to hear Mason talk anyway.

"What time is our reservation?" Masons asks, his arm anaesthetized, resting like an 'L' on the top of the couch.

"We have time, tell him."

"He was younger than me, my brother, and when he was in his mid-twenties he started hanging out with these Polish guys. Flat-faced guys named Sikorski…they also sold guns, too – mostly to the Jamaicans who'd take the Keele bus down from the god awful neighbourhoods in the north…"

Like Damon, I think.

"Anyway, one day he meets this girl on the street. He asks her out, she says yes. He came home that night very excited. I remember my father telling him to ask her questions… 'just ask her questions…ask her question and *listen* to the answers and she'll like you'…So…they go out…"

"Where did he take her?"

"The top of the Park Plaza, on Avenue Road."

"Nice," my Dad says.

"So they start to date…a couple of years go by…by this time my brother is starting to have a *difficult reaction to the world*. He's starting to go crazy…and he's walking around with a gun on him most nights. He says they were still together when it happened, but I never believed it, I think he just missed her. So…he's been drinking vodka all day with the Polacks and he takes a cab over to her place. He'd told me a couple of weeks before that he was getting obsessed with her…thinking about her too much – he was self-aware like that. It didn't make a lick of a difference, though. It never does… Anyway, I think it was actually Halloween when he went over there. He takes a cab to her place. He goes to the third floor. I really can't remember if they were together or not…I guess it doesn't matter. So, he's in front of the door and he hears cats rustling…and then of course…"

"A man's voice," my father says, and looks at me.

"Of course," Mason says. "He bangs on the door, 'open the fucking door, open the fucking door', she says, 'go away…go away'. The man is silent, all my brother can hear is the cats, right? So he takes the gun out, and fires six times through the bottom of the door. I don't think he wanted to kill them, but he wanted to make his mark. He fires through the bottom of the door and then he runs."

"Fuck," I say.

"They gave him ten years…"

I see a Chinese girl flick off her light in the bedroom across the street.

Mason looks over at my father and says "I'm getting too drunk before dinner…"

"Did he ever see the girl again?" I ask him.

He looks back at me as if he's forgotten what he was talking about. He stares at me, his eyes dark brown, trying to remember the conversation.

"Yes! Yes! Well, he said he did. He said he ran into her on a city bus. He said they went home and slept together. He said they did it in silence. But to honest, I never believed him. He'd lost it by then… poor guy…my poor brother. I'd like to see the painting before I go."

My Dad's face kind of hollows when he says that. It has reminded him of why we are here. He has forgotten, I think. The look on his face makes me feel weak.

"Right, I almost forgot about that."

I help Mason up and they move into the study.

While they're in there, I stand up and go to the window. I put my palm flat to the Christmas light that has died. It's still warm. I hear murmurings from the study, and then laughter. I text Damon a question mark and move my hand from the cool window back to the bulb, over and over until both of them feel like nothing.

I walk them outside when they're done. My silent neighbour has his slippered feet up, refuse scattered around him: a car battery, wooden blocks, some clothing suspended off the porch roof from hangers. He stares across the park. We never say anything to each other but tonight I nod. He raises his hand halfway up and resumes whatever he's thinking about. The fact that he acknowledged me makes me like him, makes me like his face. Mason and my Dad don't notice him. They step down from the stairs onto the concrete. My Dad's loafers, Mason's Velcro.

A taxi passes in front of us, the orange Vacant sign on the roof lit up, trailing towards King Street like one of those little fires people send out on the water at night. I spark a cigarette, a tiny fire much farther downriver, and lean against the short wooden fence outside our place. I raise my hand and watch them walk away.

When I'm back in the house I can see the bottle of Valium sticking out of the couch. It takes me a while to get it open, but once I do I shake three into my hand and down them with a slug of vodka.

Everything was fine with Mason's daughter until I kissed her. She was a little bit tall for me, but she was pretty and kind and liked me. On our second date, at one of those pubs on Bloor Street with the high-backed cushion booths, she got drunk and asked me if she was too tall, if she looked masculine. She didn't, of course, but the question made me like her. I kissed her after she said that.

I have a thing with girl's mouths: When they're sitting across from me and I haven't kissed them yet their mouths seem clean – like vast sparkling stainless steel tunnels. But when I do kiss them, the tunnel becomes inhabited, and of course, less appealing. More life in the tunnel, sounds from the back, smells. By the time I sleep with them it's no longer even a tunnel, it's a sewer with animals in it. Maybe it's because *I* walked through the tunnel, *all that life* materializing behind me as I move through…but maybe not.

The only girl's mouth who stayed permanently clean was Samantha's – a freshly painted glittering highway to nowhere.

I feel the little *tug, tug, tug* of the Valium and then my body goes slack. Why have I never noticed how comfortable this couch was before? And so on…

The last remnants of the hydromorph have coupled, somewhere in my nervous system, with the fresh Valium – and the result appears to be something pretty brilliant because when I open my eyes about a half an hour later, Samantha is on the couch sitting next to me. She's drinking an orange Slurpee and she's barefoot.

There is nothing *interesting* about Samantha's beauty. She looks like a fashion model, except she's short. She's wearing a purple and pink ski jacket. I ask her if she'd like to get in the bath. She drains her Slurpee and says yes. I tell her I have her shoes, I can go get them right now, they're in my room.

"But we're at my house," she says.

And we are. We're back on Grayson Street. Soft jazz music creeps from the candle-lit kitchen past the long narrow hallway with the framed photograph of her and her mother in a cornfield, towards me.

Both of them were born with that thing, that *domestic thing*. It has to do with lighting, with where you put the pillows and the way you fold a blanket before you throw it over the back of the sofa. It makes things inviting. I've seen poor girls possess it, too: a lamp shadow that hits the wall just so in a bachelor apartment in Scarborough.

I lean down and kiss her on the cheek, put my hand gently on her bum and give it a squeeze. She leads me by the hand into the bathroom. She gets in the empty tub naked and starts to run the tap – her chipped fingernail under the nozzle, making it just so. She likes to get in the empty tub and feel the water rise around her.

When the tub is filled, I put her toes in my mouth. She asks me about jail. I tell her it's boring. I ask her if she's too tired to hide tonight, she says no.

"I look in the mirror too much," she says.

"There are worse things."

"...and I laugh at things that aren't funny..."

"With me?"

"No, you're funny... You worked construction before, yeah?"

"God you are random, Samantha..."

She closes her eyes again.

"Yes, I worked construction."

"Did they have asbestos in the houses that you worked in?"

"Probably."

She closes her eyes and smiles tightly with feigned embarrassment.

"What's asbestos?"

Then she laughs.

"Asbestos is..."

I put my fingers on the outside of her, on the slit. She bites her bottom lip.

"Asbestos is a bad thing that they use to insulate stuff... it's fire-proof I think. There are lots of uses for it."

I go inside her.

"It's a bad thing...makes you sick."

She starts to breathe a little bit; in through her nose and then out through her mouth.

"Why would anyone...use it then?"

"They didn't know, I guess..."

I take my fingers out quickly so the water won't clean them. I rest them on her neck and then drag them up to her chin. It is absolutely silent in the bathroom. I've never noticed how quiet it was in there. I put my fingers in her mouth.

"Does that taste good?"

"Yuh huh," she says. "Have you ever seen it before?"

"No," I said. "I know that if it moves you're in trouble…"

I put my hand back in the bubbles and put my fingers in her body again, this time in her backside.

"Jesus fucking Christ, Hayden…"

Her neck has a little spasm and she knocks one of the shampoo bottles into the tub.

"What do you mean, if it moves you're in trouble?"

The same thing, up to her chin, into her mouth.

"What about that? Does that taste good?"

"Really good. …What do you mean, if it moves you're in trouble?"

"How good does that taste?"

"Really…rea…really good. What do you mean if it moves?"

"Let's say this bathtub was filled with asbestos – let's see these bubbles were asbestos…do you see how they're moving…breaking apart?"

I take my finger out of her mouth and point at the bubble.

"You see?"

"Yeah."

"Well, if the asbestos is doing that – it means that the fibers are coming apart…and that it's releasing the shit into the air – and that's what makes you sick."

"You should wear a mask at work," she says.

"I don't work construction anymore. Come out of the tub now, Samantha."

I get a towel and stretch it out for her so she can get into it and stay warm. I dry her breasts and her stomach and her hair and her legs.

On the walls of her basement room are black and white, nineteen-fifties-looking photographs of people kissing. She sits on her unmade bed, on top of her purple comforter. She tells me some stories about her friends, about school; all of them about seventy-eight percent true.

There is a core dishonesty to her, an overdeveloped muscle, something I always felt I was exempt from.

But Samantha, you said you were wearing your pink sweatshirt when that happened. And today you tell me you lost your pink sweatshirt years ago...

I don't know why she lies the way she does. Maybe she thinks it makes for a better story, maybe it scratches some itch, somewhere...maybe it is a mild way of hiding, the way a movie star wears sunglasses.

I never call her on it.

"I want you to count to one fifty tonight," she says.

"Why the big number?"

"I don't know...it came to me."

"Fair enough," I say.

"And I want you to quit smoking..."

"I will, soon."

I ask her what the parameters are for the evening.

"The whole house."

"It's going to take me forever to find you."

"I know," she says. "How hot is that?"

She puts her pajamas on, dark blue gingham, her dirty blonde hair still wet.

"Close your eyes now," she says.

She isn't going to be in the first closet, the one next to the boiler room, but I open it anyway. Three more of those ski jackets she wears, patterned skirts strewn across the floor, three pairs of converse and a pair of black boots. There's a worn book of poetry, dog-eared and yellow on one of the shelves next to a pamphlet on eating disorders. I open the poetry book and read the inscription.

"Stay leafy...Love, Michael."

I close it and hear the tap go upstairs. It's her mother.

I stand very still. If she talks to me it will ruin everything.

When she's gone I climb the stairs to the kitchen and check the microwave so I can tell her about it. It will make her laugh. They have a back entrance that overlooks their garden. It's more farmland than backyard – it stretches about a quarter of a mile – dark green slopes and Tiki lights covered in tarp, purple foliage shaking softly above the stone path leading to someone else's property, someone with a swimming pool. I open the backdoor quietly and smoke a cigarette on the porch. The longer she has to wait the better, the game goes both ways.

I check the closet in the laundry room behind the kitchen. It's a spot she likes. I have found her there many, many times.

Tonight there's a mop bucket, some bottles of cleaning stuff and some old Christmas ornaments in a black plastic tub. It is conceivable, given her size, that she could be under the ornaments but I don't check.

I take my shoes off at the bottom of the stairs like a ninja, like I'm doing a home invasion. I count five seconds between each step. At the top of the stairs is her mother's room, the door is slightly ajar but through the gap it is black. I listen for a second, hear nothing, and head into the study.

I know for a fact that she is not in the closet a couple of feet to my left. I would be able to hear her breathing or giggling. I walk up and put my ear to it. I hear nothing, I don't open the door, it's too close to her mother's room to gamble. If she's not in the attic I can always come back down.

The roof of the attic is a triangle, and there's a skylight outlined in blue duct tape. I hear her chuckle when I step onto the hardwood floors.

"Samantha…" I whisper.

I open the closet. The smell of her hits me immediately, like a softer form of chlorine.

Here at the Jane and Falstaff community centre we clean our pools with "Samantha."

She's crouched down, holding her knees – under her bum is a mass of blue winter coats. She stares up at me and smiles. She has a bandana across her forehead; either she's found it in the closet or she's been wearing it all day.

When I find her she likes me to slap her or put my hands around her throat. It was jarring at first, but she liked it and so I liked it.

I stand there for a second deciding between the two, watching her wrapped in her blue coats as if she were underwater.

I don't slap her tonight. I don't put my arms around her small neck, or spit on her, or anything like that.

I get into the closet with her and shut the door, the blue coats under my bum now, too.

We sit there in silence for a couple of minutes; she reaches her hand out and lays it across my chest.

"Your heart is beating fast," she says. "And you smell bad…"

I laugh in the dark. Her face looks wild in there, in the dark, the light from under the door, the light from outside, from down the block, from another planet, resting on her cheekbones. Her eyes looking like an old woman's.

I've had three years to construct a sentence that will let her know, concisely, how fucked I am without her. I have practiced it hundreds of times. In front of the mirror, on my way home from the convenience store though the sharp, ugly night.

I have recited it in many languages.

Now that she is here, though, I can't think of anything interesting to say.

"I miss you, Samantha," I say.

She nods.

TEN P.M.

I wake up to those things buzzing – those things I can't remember the name of. I get up off the couch and go upstairs and lie down on my bed. I slap myself quickly across the face to make sure I'm awake. I check my phone – nothing from Damon. I look over at Samantha's running shoes. I have been dreaming for too long.

I say it out loud.

"I have been dreaming too long."

I get up off the bed and look at myself in the mirror. Then I take the running shoes and put them under my arm and go back downstairs. I head out the front door barefoot and place her shoes softly on the front porch of the abandoned house.

☙

Shortly after my high school graduation Damon brought me to a house party in the north end of the city. He periodically made friends with the decadent, animal-faced rich boys who frequented after-hours bars – guys who liked blow and tequila and massage parlors despite all the hockey equipment they had in their basements as tykes. He'd hook up with them for a little while and then go back to hanging out with the Jamaicans up on Falstaff or the Italians on St. Clair. He was a traveler, Damon. He'd been selling drugs and wandering around Toronto, his inner power increasing, his arrest record growing, since he was fourteen years old.

To this day I have a bit of silly pride that I was the only one he was ever truly friends with.

We spent the day at his apartment watching horse racing, me doing small lines of Oxycontin, him drinking beer and smoking weed.

When we got to the house party and stood in front of it, the summer heat on our faces, the blue Christmas lights they'd put up reflecting off Damon's neck, I passed him a drag of my cigarette.

"My Dad puts up Christmas lights in the summer, too," I said.

I saw Samantha at the corner of the party but didn't speak to her. She had her hair in two short braids and she was smoking a thin cigar in front of the table with chips and liquor on it. Her jaw was twitching softly and there were two guys talking to her – both tall. She looked at one of them with intrigue, and the other with disdain, back and forth like that – very honest.

I watched her until she noticed me.

At around midnight Damon pretended to throw up in the bathroom. He locked himself in and about a half an hour later his friends showed up with guns and made everybody – mascara-eyed girls in cocktail dresses and sweet-faced guys in sweater vests – carry stereos and DVD players into the U-haul that was parked outside. She came and stood next to me while it was happening. I whispered in her ear that she didn't have to carry anything.

"You're too little."

Despite everything, she chuckled when I said that.

As the last of the electronic equipment made its way into the van, I took Samantha by the hand and led her out into the backyard. I asked her if she remembered me from Grayson Street – she said no. She told me she liked that I was tall, though. We made our way around the side gate, but as we were leaving I felt a gloved hand on my shoulder. It was a work glove.

I turned around and saw one of Damon's goons. He had a toque on and bandana under his chin. He had a fat acne-scarred nose and yellow skin. I knew who he was, Damon had let it slip that he didn't like me. He didn't like "junkies." Unintelligent criminals don't like drug addicts. They say it's because they're weak and untrustworthy but that's bullshit. They don't like them because they're smarter and have a certain shine to them. That certain shine is charm and good luck. The smart ones, like Damon, like them and keep them around. That is, until that charm is just a shell and the hunger overrides.

He looked jaundiced but excited. He asked me to stay in the house until the job was done. I told him to fuck off and continued around the side of the house with Samantha. When I turned around at the last minute he was still standing there, arms crossed, grinning.

She told me her parents were out of town and so we hopped in a taxi to Grayson Street.

She had one of those houses that looked like no one lived there: the living room with the expensive high-backed chairs and the coffee table with books on famous floods and German paintings.

Spotlessly clean.

She got me a gleaming coke out of the fridge. Rich people always had coke in the fridge, like twenty cans of it. They kept the back-ups in the basement. The cans didn't look as good down there in the dark, all packaged up in dusty plastic.

I asked her where her room was. She told me to relax. She poured the rest of her coke into her glass. I put my hand on the side of her face and brushed her hair behind her ear. She turned around and put her hand on my shoulder and kissed me. I put my hand up her shirt. She took it out of my pants and put her hand on it.

"Nice," she said.

"Yeah?"

She nodded.

"Why does your house look like no one lives in it?"

She had glow-in-dark stars and moons on the ceiling above her bed. Some were scraped off. You could tell she'd tried to scrape them off but had given up halfway through.

When it was done, she stood naked at the bay windows in her room and said my name in a breathy, hurried whisper. Like we were underwater together, and she'd lost sight of me for just a moment.

When I got home I noticed there was something wrong with the lighting in the house. It was dark except for a gold accountant's lamp switched on in the corner of the living room next to his easel. He'd inherited the lamp from his mother but mostly it stayed lifeless next to his cowboy boots in the closet. It was the first time I'd ever seen it turned on. It made the house look sick.

I sat down on the couch and closed my eyes. I thought about Samantha sleeping in the fog of her room, her mouth slightly open, and then about Yellow Skin at the house party – the way he grinned at me. Eventually the two thoughts merged and he was standing over her watching, trying to sync up his breath with hers.

I took out my phone and called Damon. When he picked up I told him that if that guy ever told me what to do again I'd break his jaw. He didn't even respond to that one. He asked me what I'd done with my night. I told him, semi-cautiously, about Samantha. I knew not to get too detailed, to keep it special, but Damon was cool that way – he could rise to the occasion. We talked about basketball after that.

I always liked the image of him that evening – a job completed, safe and sound smoking weed under his blanket in his tiny bachelor apartment at Sherbourne and Dundas, the sports channel flickering away.

It made me sad, too – there was an independence to it that seemed ungraspable to me. His days involved him and his need to make money, and since he'd made money not just for the day but for the month, his time was his.

We said goodnight and then I hung up the phone. I was about to get up and go into the kitchen to get a beer when I saw him come up the basement stairs.

I knew, at that moment, that we had *arrived somewhere.* He didn't look at me, he walked slowly through the kitchen into the living room, his eyes on the floor, and when he was about two feet away he kicked the television over. He did it violently but I didn't move. If anything, it made me stiller. It's funny how you get used to that stuff…

He looked down at the toppled television and breathed heavily for just a couple of seconds too long. There was a self-consciousness to those final seconds, I noticed. He was close enough to take my oxygen at that point, and was feeling better already, I could tell.

He pushed on, though…

"I want to die!" he yelled. "I want to die and you have to help me!"

"Dad, you can't do this shit…you know that."

He sat down on the floor and put his head in his hands. I watched his shoulders go up and down, confused as to how I felt so calm, but proud too.

After a while he apologized and I put my hand on him.

"What is you want, Dad? What is it?"

"My life," he said…"think of my life as a shower, and the shower walls, on the outside, are just smeared with grey shit. Grey…fucking…shit. And the shit is on the outside…so I cannot…wipe the shit off…and it blinds me. I'm blinded by it…you know?"

I had a quarter of an Oxycontin in my pocket so I gave it to him. He downed it dry and we went into my room. He said sorry a bunch more times and lay on the floor next to my bed. We talked about going on a vacation. I listed off countries and he responded with yes, or he didn't respond at all. We lay silent after that.

I heard him get up when the Oxy clicked in, then the television lifted back up and turned on in the living room.

Living with a guy like that, over the years, he's going to take some things, sure.

Oxygen, experience.

Until that night, though, it always felt like collateral damage – a side-effect of *us*. Things got fucked up, he was a troubled guy.

There would be other school trips, other Halloweens, there would come a time when he would leave my head.

Poof, just like that.

These thinned experiences of mine – the ones tainted by his presence or by the shading of his absence, I looked at as offerings, but in the end unimportant offerings. I was young, after all, I had my whole life ahead of me. He was my father, I loved him – and more importantly, I liked him.

It wasn't until that night, in those final seconds before sleep, that I realized this dissipated oxygen, these amputated sections of my spirit, weren't just dissolving randomly into space – they were going to him.

And they didn't feel unlimited like they had in the past. I was getting older.

It was malicious but *he* wasn't malicious. I mean, if anything he was unaware of it; his need to survive was blind… whatever had to happen, had to happen as long as he got the hit – the hit that night being Samantha.

A big hit.

Because, if there was ever a smell, in the history of the world, that *suggested life*, it was hers.

And so it felt, for the first time, that we actually met each other that evening. Two strangers wandering onto the same vacant, cobblestone patio sat by the waiter at the only table in the joint that wasn't slanted…a cigar for both of us, drinks all around and…well, I'd finally found something I wasn't going to part with.

He was trying to take Samantha's smell from me, and so at some point while I dreamt, while the Christmas lights blinked away downstairs, something agile passed over my sleeping, twenty year old body and evaporated soundlessly, making me bolt upright and exhale.

The need for it was so fresh I felt like a different person. I wanted him to die.

I was getting older.

ɔ઩

His legs are dangling off the side of the counter in the kitchen when I come downstairs. He's smoking a joint. I stand in the doorframe and watch him stare at the black and white checkered floor tile. He curls the smoke out of his mouth and up into his nose. The joint is rolled in cheap cigar paper. He's the only guy I know his age who smokes blunts like that – Damon showed him.

"I want you to tell me three things that you liked about me being your father," he says.

I list off three quickly.

"Not hard to come up with three," I say.

He takes a small puff from the joint and lays it beside him so the lit part is hanging freely off the edge. I can see the horses on his socks now.

"Do you remember when I told you *to tell me* if you started to have an *adverse reaction* to my presence?"

He picks up the joint and offers it to me.

"No thanks, Dad. I hate that shit."

"You do, don't you. It makes you…"

"Paranoid – makes me want to hide under the couch. What does it do to you?"

He coughs.

"Just mellows me out, man."

He dabs some spit on his index finger and outs the joint.

"Mellows me right the fuck out…do you remember when I asked you that?"

"Yeah," I say.

He pushes himself off the kitchen counter with his palms and stands by the window.

"Sometimes there are these people, and you love them, but too many things have happened...and your body...your body remembers these things – so you see them and you just get kind of bummed out...you know?""

I nod.

"You were a nice guy about it, you said no. Of course you said no..."

His eyes water a little bit and his mouth goes kind of slack. He puts a hand out and leans on the window.

"I was thinking, though, that by the time I asked you that...by the time I asked you that question, it had already happened."

He turns around and fills the martini glasses with hot water to soak them. He leaves the three of them sitting together on the counter and goes back to the window. I go over and stand next to him. The street is empty – his blazer looks rumpled now, he's wearing expensive grey jeans that I helped him pick out for Christmas one year. I must have been eight or nine. We stayed at a massive green hotel in Florida and watched *Scarface* and ordered pizza. I remember him telling me there were alligators in the ocean. I don't know why, but I found it very funny, and he kept saying it, and I kept laughing.

It made me laugh, and he kept saying it over and over again. I don't know why it made me laugh so hard.

"What's Damon up to tonight?" he asks me.

I don't say anything.

He repeats.

"Maybe he shouldn't come," I say.

"Oh...I think he should. I think you'll regret that in the morning, son."

He's only called me son on three occasions: when I graduated high school, when I got arrested for the first time, and just now.

I sit down at the high table in our kitchen, take a cigarette out and tap it on the wood.

"Do you ever think about having children?" he asks me.

"With who?" I say.

He pauses for a second.

"With Samantha."

This surprises me. There's something ballsy about the way he says her name, the way he looks me right in the eye when he does it, that makes me smile. He's been afraid of me for the last year. It's something I've liked in a hollow kind of way – couldn't help but like it. He's told me on a few occasions that he wakes up in the middle of the night and runs through everything "disgraceful" he's ever done as a father. When he told me that all I could focus on was that he used the word "disgraceful," which seemed like a faggy, bullshit word to use. That's where we were.

By saying her name like that, though, by bringing up the fantasy of our reconciliation so casually, by *shattering the preciousness* of Samantha's ghost, he's letting me know he's not afraid of me. And if he's not afraid of me he's not afraid of the past and if he's not afraid of the past…well, shit, he's not afraid of anything.

Which means he's close, he's ready to go. There's something solid about it that makes me want to hug him. He smiles back at me when I smile. Neither of us needs to say anything.

"How is that going to happen, Dad?"

His eyes squint.

"Because you're going to get her back," he says.

I flip my cigarette around and start tapping it from the other end.

I wait a couple of seconds and then ask him straight: "How?"

"I have no fucking idea, Hayden. But you will."

And I respond honestly, I respond with:

"You know I got her pregnant once?'

"No, you never told me that."

I ask him if I can smoke a cigarette inside. He nods and gets me an ashtray out of the cupboard. It has a painting of the green hotel in the centre.

"I was worried I was going to think about it for a longer time…when it happened. But I've forgotten about it, kind of…I never thought it would hit me like that – I always thought I'd be pretty casual about it. But when she told me it had a little heart-beat already…that fucked me up. And that's cheesy, I know. But that's what it was that fucked me up."

"How was *she* about it?"

"She was cool, the coolest girl in there. There was one in there, she had this tight ponytail, this look on her face – her boyfriend was freaked right the fuck out. You knew…you just knew…that he was going to pay for that forever…girl loosens up for one night and look what happened…"

He half-laughs. He's somewhere else now.

I pick up the ashtray with my smoldering cigarette in it. "You remember?"

"I remember…you liked it there, didn't you?"

"I did. I have dreams about it still…"

"I think I have to lie down, Hayden…"

My phone goes off. Damon.

Hour later, sorry duke.

"Don't lie down, Dad. Let's go out."

"Damon's going to be here soon…and I just want to lie down for a little bit."

I tell him that Damon's just texted, that he's going to be an hour later.

When I say that he turns around and opens the cupboard, first slowly, and then with a slam. He takes a mug and smashes it on the checkered floor and yells something.

He looks at me and says sorry.

"That's fine, man. It's fine."

"It's just…Hayden, like, fuck man, if we're going to do it, let's do it, you know?"

"Dad, let's go out. I want to show you something, you'll like it."

"No, no…this dog's staying on the porch. Fucking Damon, fucking around…"

"Come on let's go, let's bring the vodka and let's go."

He's usually effusively nice to cab drivers but tonight he sits quietly in the dark. The cab driver wants to chat about the weather, how beautiful it's been, but I say, "If you don't mind, we're not feeling great tonight…we're up not to chat, if you don't mind."

He flicks the radio on, one of those soft jazz stations with the guys with the deep voice, the guys underwater.

And tonight we have something very special…very, very special…I heard this as a young man and it came to me the other day so I thought I would share it with you all…

We move along Queen Street, past the clothing stores and the hotdog stands, the owners on a stool in their little box, next to their little lights. A couple of girls in jeans outside of a bar just closing, going home. Happy to be going home…a night completed. Back to work in the morning.

Isn't that something?

As we approach Parkdale I start to worry about who is going to pay for the cab. I get an image of neither of us having any cash, the driver locking the door and driving us to a police station.

It happened before at a friend's funeral. Italian kid, Michael Amatulli – I spent the entire service worrying if I'd put on deodorant, not, if people could smell me, if they were going to talk about it.

It's just perversity, neuroses. The kitchen sink overflowing because the one in the basement is blocked.

"You know what we used to call short girls when I was your age?"

"Spinners?"

He laughs, so does the cab driver.

"Yeah, spinners."

"We call them spinners, too."

When we pull up in front of the Shawarma place he takes a twenty dollar bill from the inside of his blazer and hands it to the driver. He hands me the change, three toonies, and takes the vodka bottle from where his feet are. He steps out of the cab and shuts the door. I watch him through the window. His blazer looks better now. I hand the driver a toonie.

He puts his hand on my shoulder and we walk. Usually I don't like when he does it on the street, it sounds stupid but I get worried people will think we're gay or something. Tonight I don't mind it.

He uncorks the bottle of Stoli and takes a swig. Two white kids in tight jeans, striped t-shirts and baseball hats walk by us. The cab makes a u-turn and escapes down a side street.

"I remember when all you guys wore baggy pants," he says. "What happened to that?"

"It changed, I guess," I say. "I don't like it much."

"Yeah, but the pants fit now…"

"I don't know…I don't like it as much…"

The house is being rebuilt with that fresh unpainted yellow wood. We stand in front of it, passing the vodka bottle back and forth. There's a tarp where the new window will be.

I put on Damon's voice as I'm preparing to say it, a black guy's drawl.

"You see that shit, Dad? I burned that shit down… dowwwnnn…"

☙

One night I caught her praying in the bathroom – her hands clasped over the toilet seat. I'd never seen anyone pray before. At first I thought it was a joke. Like she was going to turn around and grin and say "gotcha!"

I was bartending the lunch shift at a sports bar on College Street at the time. They had pictures of Sylvester Stallone everywhere – not movie shots, they looked like personal photographs. Sly outside of a barn, Sly next to the refrigerator...

It was weird.

My shift ended around the time she finished school (she was taking philosophy at York) and so almost every day after work I'd step out into the street with a pocketful of money and there she'd be on the patio, her green knapsack on the chair next to her, her hair in braids, smoking a cigarette and drinking something orange and sticky and glowing. The Portuguese guys would stare at her.

We'd go all over the city. We'd go to High Park or to Scarborough – anywhere we hadn't been before. It didn't matter, as long as it wasn't Chinatown or Yonge and Eglinton. We'd find parks, usually. We'd find parks and kiss. Sometimes we'd get drunk, but mostly we'd just kiss. She had a way of touching me that calmed things. It made me light-headed, dizzy almost.

She was fashionable to the point of artistry, she believed "solar flares" were responsible for my headaches, she was decadent the way a child is decadent: she liked to play Mario Kart and eat pizza until it stopped giving her pleasure.

She understood male sexuality as if she were a guy, the simplicity of it – that at its core, it was about defiling something seemingly delicate.

I never told her about the fire I lit the night I met her.

She had a strange reaction to cocaine. She only did it occasionally but when she did it would always end up the same way: her jaw twitching, her sweaty fingers on the cell phone trying to get another bag at ten o'clock in the morning, the birds chirping outside, the screen door of her house banging shut as the mailman left.

When all the money was gone she'd start looking on the floor. She called it "carpet surfing." Damon had told me he'd seen crack heads do it but I'd never heard of anyone doing it with coke. I mean, what exactly did she think she was going to find down there?

She told me one morning, a little bit sheepish, but not *that* sheepish, that it had nothing to do with finding anything – it was the searching that was important, it passed the time, made the comedown easier.

Damon was selling me one Oxycontin per week at that point. That was the limit he set for me. No matter how much I'd bug him he'd never sell me more than one a week. We weren't spending that much time with each other, anyway. Sometimes he'd make insinuations about Samantha – when we finally had it out he told me he was just pissed off I hadn't been around as much.

The fourth time I saw her down on the floor in her mother's basement I gave her half an Oxy. There was white stuff at the corners of her mouth and her jaw was twitching so violently I thought she was going to have a heart attack. I wanted her to sleep.

I gave her half a pink twenty and told her to chew it so it would hit faster. She refused at first. She said we should try to trade it for another bag of coke. I laughed and looked around the basement.

"To who?"

Finally she took it. Forty five minutes later we went to the grocery store and bought the stuff you need to make lasagna.

I'd stopped speaking to my father completely.

I was living on Grayson Street with Samantha and her mother and I'd stopped picking up his phone calls. Sometimes shards of guilt would pass through me so raggedly I'd be unable to get out of bed for hours. I'd smoke ten cigarettes in the dark and then it would pass, then he would leave my mind.

We rarely fought. We had a couple of little spats. Once, during a game of Monopoly, I made a crack about one of her friends. I'd mocked the girl's use of the term "work ethic" (while speaking about herself) as it applied to her three-class course load in political science and her after-school job picking up mats at a yoga studio. We got into a little bit. She was deeply loyal to her handful of girlfriends, and it was a stupid thing to say, but, even though we'd been together a while – I was flirting, trying to get a rise out of her. When someone's that beautiful you're always trying to *get them.*

We made up in about ten minutes, at which point she asked me to sodomize her – so I did, right there in the kitchen.

It was nice. Samantha, as you can imagine, had a very small asshole.

After that, she put on her curiously beat-up gym clothes and went for a run. I cleaned up the board, put the shoe and the hat back in the box and sat there thinking about her until she got back. She returned wet faced and dry mouthed, a small dark stain the size of a quarter above her right hip.

She stood in the doorway that led out into the backyard, panting softly, the summer night behind her, eyes wide, the faint murmurings of the music she'd been listening to coming through the headphones draped over her shoulder. She said nothing, she just stared at me.

By listening to the faded music, it was as if I'd been allowed access to something – some part of her internal life, of her subconscious – as if her most private thoughts were still trapped in the song, and I could hear them, or at least the buzzing of the world they existed in.

It made my heart beat quickly, and I've never forgotten it. I fell in love with her.

Damon's apartment got raided near the end of the summer. They found two ounces of cocaine. He'd had a pistol, too, but he'd thrown it out the window in a brown paper bag when he'd seen them on the television. Like most shithole apartment buildings, you could see the lobby's security surveillance on channel 192.

He got out a couple of months later, the charges dismantled by his lawyer until they were nothing. You can get away with a lot in Canada.

He pulled up in front of Samantha's house in December while I was shoveling the snow. He was blind drunk and being driven around in a purple PT Cruiser by a Ukrainian girl. It was the first time I'd seen him since he'd got out. He had half of his red hair in corn rows and the other half an afro.

He gave me a little hug through the window and handed me a couple of pills. He told me we'd meet up the next day – that he'd missed me. I looked over at the blonde to monitor if she'd recognized the sweetness of this – she hadn't.

I'd quit the bartending job by that point and so I'd spent the week ripping hundreds of nails out of a third floor attic with a hammer. The trick to mindless *and* physically difficult work is to not burn yourself out – you look at the planks, hundreds of them, and you just want to power through it, get it done – but you have to do one board at a time or you'll fuck your back up. The Jamaicans taught me that. My father taught me that, too.

When I got back inside, with the pills in my pocket, she was pouring two glasses of wine on the marble island in the middle of the kitchen: black jeans, one shoulder hanging out of her tank top. She was trying to fill the glasses the same. I went up behind her and kissed her head.

I told her she smelled nice, she asked me if I liked blues. I said sure, she put on some blues.

She'd developed a way of speaking, a British thing, she lifted "side" at the end when she said "let's go outside."

Her backyard turned dark green at night and the Tiki lights were covered in black plastic and dusted with snow. The trees blocked out the sky almost completely. Purple leaves.

It was dusk when she put on her lip gloss. She smoked half of my cigarette and exhaled it towards the tops of the trees.

We talked about my job, about school, about her father, how when he'd left he'd said: "I will do anything to never see your mother again, even if it means not seeing you, whom I love so very, very much."

We'd decided to have another glass of wine and then go downstairs to her basement and watch a movie. A comedy, I think.

I took the pills out of my pocket and put them on the table.

"He's back?" she said.

About half an hour later, I lit a cigarette and found, while I was exhaling, the experience of the smoke hitting my throat to be completely and totally satisfying. I could exhale it any number of ways, but any way would be sufficient – just fine, as long as the smoke was exhaled. It felt good to squint, but if I didn't want to squint…that would be just fine, too.

She asked to feel my arms. Then asked why it felt like we'd just met each other.

The trees shook above us, it was getting colder.

I asked her to come sit next to me. After a second or two she got out of her chair and sat on my lap. She scrunched up her body so her entire weight was on me. Her eyes, her hyena eyes, tiny and blue and slanted, were pinned out and she looked like a different person.

I told her I loved her and then we went inside and we prayed. We got down on our knees and clasped our hands over the cushions of her cream-coloured sofa.

"You should pray for your father," she said.

"Nah, he'd think it was stupid…"

"He won't hear it…"

"Yeah, he will."

Twelve A.M.

He slugs the vodka back and looks at the house, passes me the bottle.

"Why?"

"Just mellows me out, Dad. Mellows me right the fuck out..."

He doesn't laugh, and I feel the drugs wearing off. He repeats.

"Why?"

"Same reason you paint, I guess..."

I pass him the bottle back.

"What was this place?"

"An after-hours bar..."

He takes his fingers and rubs them across his chest, downwards across the middle of blazer, his index finger on his t-shirt.

"I'm guessing that's what you were planning to do on our block, at the house?"

"Before that faggot cop fucked it up, yeah..."

"Don't be harsh, Hayden...don't be harsh when you speak like that..."

"Okay."

He pauses.

"Why?"

"I just told you."

"Me?"

"Sure."

"Samantha?"

"Sure."

"You hate me?"

"No."

"Weren't you worried someone was going to get hurt?"

"I knew the place was empty..."

"Yeah, but other things can happen. Firemen can get killed…"

He lets that sit in the air for a second.

"I don't know what to tell you," I say. "I knew what I was doing. I know what I'm doing."

He sets the vodka bottle on the ground with a small clink.

"It was scarier, the idea of not doing it…I know I sound crazy but that's the truth."

He stops himself from pressing it further.

"It's all very interesting," he says.

He looks over at me.

"You know you liked fire as a little boy…I used to let you light the candles when we had dinner. You liked that a lot."

Headlights that seem *sharper* than usual pass behind us; they illuminate our legs. He doesn't notice.

೮೪

In June one night, I came home from work and her mother was standing on the front porch in a rain jacket smoking a cigarette. She looked kind of sexy, her hair matted, her eyes dim. She told me she was sending Samantha to rehab in California. The place cost twenty thousand dollars. She was leaving in three days. I asked if I could go upstairs and see her. No, she was sleeping. I had to leave, *now*.

I still remember the consecutive amount of raindrops vibrating through my work fleece when it hit me.

I wandered around for a little while and then I went back to my father's. I hadn't seen him, or spoken to him, for more than a year. I passed the abandoned house on the way up my old street. Our door was open.

He was sitting on the couch in his boxers with one sock on, *The X Files* on television. He looked okay, he had colour in his face and the house was clean. There was a poster of Britney Spears in a schoolgirl's uniform on the wall in the kitchen.

I told him what had happened; he nodded like he already knew.

I asked him what was going to happen to me, now that she was gone.

"Of course it's raining, right?" he said.

I went into the kitchen and made myself a pop tart – then I went back into the living room and asked him if he wanted to paint me.

He said, as we moved into this study, that he had taken nine sleeping pills and drunk eight beers – and for the first time, in a long time, he felt really good.

I went by Damon's after and told him what happened. He was out of Oxycontin but he had a small Ziploc bag of Percodan. He sold me all of them. He hadn't, until that day, broken his rule about the pills: Samantha and I had been double dipping, buying them off a cancer patient up at Pape and Cosburn in addition to Damon's allowance.

I did six on the spot, watched horse-racing for a bit, and went to the convenience store on the corner of his street before I got into a taxi.

I knew, when I got to the Greyhound station, that if I didn't eat soon I was going to get into a fight. The percs, while I'd done a lot of them, were filled with acetaminophen and other shit, and so there was this unavoidable gap between the chalky white pills and what I was used to taking (seven clean forty milligram Oxycontin a week, five for Samantha).

The gap made me irritable. I couldn't quite get to the water.

Next to the long, connected row of beige chairs was a hamburger stand. I could smell the meat searing. There was a line up, a row of school kids, mostly Asian. They were laughing and dancing and feeding each other fries. I stared at the kids, half-hoping their joy would change me and half waiting for them to hurry the fuck up.

I thought to myself, I'm going to have a cigarette, and then I'm going to have my hamburger, and then I'm going to buy my ticket. No, I'm going to have my hamburger first and then my cigarette because it will feel better, and then buy my ticket – maybe I should just get on the fucking bus right now, no that's stupid, you'll be starving and you didn't even buy any water to chase the percs down – okay, the lineup must be done by now, you can't even hear the kids, well, to be sure you could open your eyes and you can see. Just open your eyes; it's as simple as that, Hayden. Open your eyes. For fuck's sakes man, you opened them and you didn't even look up to see if…everything must be marked. Good luck.

It was midnight when I woke up. The hamburger stand was closed. A pair of Pakistani women a couple of seats down smiled at me. I smiled back. I remembered the percs and slammed my palms against the breast pocket of my jacket to make sure they were still there. They were.

There had been, six hours before, eight caged booths across from me – attendants in each. Now all were closed except for one. But one was good enough.

I bought a ticket north and did another pill, then went to the McDonalds across the street and ate six cheeseburgers, watching my reflection in the yellowish window until I saw a bus pull in.

I've always loved being on a bus at night, the trees moving all quickly like that – the moon rolling backwards, the brick farmhouses (who *lives* there?).

After an hour or so it pulled over and let three gentle figures off – all bundled up and warm. I closed my eyes and waited for the movement to start again but it didn't. When I looked up, the driver was gone. I walked softly through the aisle, my feet hitting the filthy patterned carpet, and stepped into the cold air. He was smoking a cigarette and wearing a fedora, his back to me, gazing ahead at the miles and miles of leaning, silver cornfield. At the very edge of what I could see in the distance, where the sky hit the ground, was a black vertical shape.

Maybe an outhouse.

I stood next to him and lit a cigarette. On his Greyhound shirt the name *Harley* was stitched in pink cursive lettering. He was in his mid-thirties, handsome, and had tattoos creeping out from under his sleeves. I had a feeling he only put his hat on when he got far away enough from the terminal.

He said, the cigarette hanging out of his mouth, "You know what I like about the country? You can watch your dog run away for three days…"

I nodded and we stood there, the both of us, smoking and staring.

We talked for a couple of minutes – I told him my girlfriend had broken up with me. I got the reaction I wanted – good old-fashioned surface commentary, as if I were describing a comic book, a different girl even.

He turned back and squinted when I didn't follow him back onto the bus. I told him someone was coming to get me. He paused for a second and then let it go.

The doors closed but it didn't move right away. And then it did – it rolled forward and was gone. I hopped over the little wire fence and my feet hit the cornfield. It must have been one o'clock in the morning.

As I walked, I thought about the afternoon I'd gotten her pregnant. She'd been on her period and as I'd pulled away from her body I'd brushed up against her leg, leaving what looked like a tiny red handprint branded on her inner thigh. I knew then that it had happened, despite the way girl's systems worked.

As I got closer to the black vertical shape, it started to take form – it wasn't rectangular and vertical like I'd thought – it was pyramid-shaped, and covered lazily in canvas. Nothing behind it but stars and flatness and night.

The tarp was thick and heavy but it wasn't bolted to anything. When I finally tore it away and left it crooked in the field I saw what was underneath:

Twelve bales of hay, wrapped in dotted twine, about four feet by four feet each, one on top of the other – in a pyramid.

Right, I thought.

I laid the tarp flat on the snow and sat down on it – the pyramid above me. I closed my eyes and tried to cry but I couldn't. Each time the release seemed to approach, the percs would click in and I'd be brought back to the wind on my face, and how lovely that felt. Eventually I gave up and climbed to the top of the pyramid.

I took the flask out of my work fleece and, kneeling down, doused the top with the fluid – the liquid darkening the brown, the action feeling excessive (because it was).

I put a lighter to it – and then as quickly as I could, jumped down and did the same at the bottom, leaping backwards onto the tarp so I wouldn't miss anything.

There was a barn about five miles east. All I had to do was make it to that.

It took a while, just smoke at first, but then whispers of gold and heliotrope started to move through and it became animate...like a yeti, who after ignoring his many calls home, had self-immolated out on the tundra.

In fragments, though:

First a thin cap of flame, and then ankles that erupted as well. I watched it travel upwards and downwards, flaring at the abdomen and the shoulders, and finally the neck and feet.

The flames fed into each other, chased each other.

I liked the way it smelled – it was the correct thing. I knew this like I knew I was blonde, or I was male, or that Samantha...

As it burned, motionless, the memory of Samantha and me became translucent...not the world we lived in, but us, our bodies. We were translucent. The idea that people *met*...I'd never looked at it like that. People met, they came together. Jesus.

I lay down. I thought about lying there until the fire died...but I knew better than that...I knew, as long as it burned I'd stay in this zone...and the minute it was done, it would all start up.

I'd start missing her.

The smoke had made the stars blur. I started to walk. I kept looking back and looking back and every time I did it was still burning, static, at attention.

It must have been five o'clock in the morning when I got to the barn. There were two full garbage bags in the corner. I went to the opposite wall, as far away from them as possible, and fell asleep.

The barn was empty and quiet when I woke up. I opened the double doors to look outside – it was gone, I couldn't even see the black in the snow. I did the last two percs and untied one of the garbage bags. I tossed the lighter fluid inside and tied it back up again.

As I walked towards the highway the percs began to click, and the terror of waking up alone like that started to subside.

Once I got some cigarettes, I'd be okay.

It started to rain again on my way back into the city. I arrived on Grayson Street at three o'clock in the afternoon, my jacket drenched, still smelling like smoke.

I realized when I rung the bell how dirty my fingernails were. The rain hadn't done anything to them – if anything it had made them dirtier.

Samantha's mother answered the door. She took one look at me and told me to come in.

She took my jacket into the basement to throw in the dryer and when she came back up she put her arms around me.

She told me she's always liked me – she said I'd always *calmed Samantha down.*

For whatever reason I've always remembered that.

She was sleeping when I came into her room, the painting of Miles Davis with a frozen trumpet above the bed.

I got into bed next to her, kissed her back and her legs and her bum for a little. When she was half awake we made love. Her breath smelled terrible, but I didn't care.

She said, when it was over, "I feel soo…fuckkingg…terribble…in my stomach, my bones…"

She asked me why I didn't get sick.

"I don't think I took as many as you."

"I think it's because you're so strong," she said sleepily, "So strong and…so handsome."

She put her hand on the side of my face and then she looked at me.

I'd see it manifest itself differently over the years, but it was the first time I saw the foreign twinkle in the eye of someone who'd moved on. The dope hadn't left her body yet, but it had, in a matter of days, become a part of the past.

And me with it.

"Can I sleep in bed with you today…and tonight?" I asked her.

"Of course you can. But I have to wake up so early in the morning, fuck…"

But I still don't understand…what morning?

☙

The same headlights again – this time coming from a different direction.

"I don't believe you, Hayden. All this "making my mark" shit…I don't believe it. I think you should tell me the truth… think you should tell me the truth. You owe me that. I know you don't think you do, but you do…you owe me."

"I don't owe you anything," I say.

I look at him; he has a kind of bemused look on his face, like he's interrogating a hapless young offender.

I repeat it.

"Absolutely nothing."

The headlights have slowed now, a silver Acura reverses and pulls up onto the curb behind us. It sits still for a second. My dad looks back disinterestedly – like it's a screaming baby in a shopping mall, just a nuisance. The door opens slowly and a thick-looking guy in a black varsity jacket with "Darlene" stitched into the breast gets out. He has blonde hair like me but it's slicked over his forehead and across the back of his neck and he's wearing glasses and shiny brown dress shoes.

He doesn't recognize me but we've met before. He'd come by Damon's one time with a couple of girls he was pimping out. Eventually the girls, *his* girls, started teasing him – rustling his hair, calling him a pussy – this went on until Damon kicked all of them out for freebasing in the living room.

"You've got to be cold-blooded to run girls, man, to do it properly...homie just doesn't have it in him..."

A girl gets out of the passenger seat. She's dressed like an off-duty stripper; the immaculate grey hoodie, the expensive yoga pants, the furry boots. She's harsh-looking at first but her eyes go wide and sweet when she looks at us. It's like she can't help it. Can't help but be sweet.

So he's found a nice one, I think.

The guy nods, the girl looking at him, back to us, back to him again.

"What are you boys up to?"

He says it so quietly it doesn't register for a couple of seconds.

He crosses his hands over his jeans like a waiter during a slow shift, trying to look attentive.

"What happened here?" my Dad says.

"How the fuck should I know? What are you boys up to?"

My Dad motions to the almost empty vodka bottle on the ground.

"I'm having a drink with my son, what does it look like?"

He winces when my Dad says that. The girl pulls out a long cigarette, lights it and blows it lazily out the side of her mouth – it's bullshit, though, she's nervous.

"I need you guys to move along now – my boss owns this property, we just want to make sure we don't have any more problems…if you guys don't mind, just move along…"

Violent guys with glasses are always interesting to watch; like some benignly ugly insect – you never expect it but when it comes it's always bad.

My Dad spits out the side of his mouth and says, "Why don't you get back in your car?"

"Excuse me, brother?"

"Why don't you get back in your fucking car, you fucking goof…and when you get home, I want you to go home and suck your mother…you understand me?"

Calling someone a "goof" and telling them to "go and suck your mother" are the two big no-no's in jail. The "go" words. Guaranteed fight. Damon taught him that.

The guy chuckles self-consciously. What my Dad's said has shocked him, but *the way* he's said it has shocked him more.

"You've been in the pen, partner?"

"No, but my son has."

Obviously I haven't been to the pen but the girl shoots me a look when he says that and so I like it. I'm starting to get a feeling our friend hasn't been to the pen, either.

Varsity jacket looks at me for a second and then back at my Dad.

"You're putting me in a bad position now, brother. I'm with a girl, you can see that can't you? Where's your fucking decency?"

He looks back at me.

"This your old man? Where's his fucking decency?"

My Dad steps a foot closer to him, and when he does, the empty vodka bottle topples over and clinks to the curb, over it, and underneath the car. The girl watches it roll.

The girl says, her eyes still on the ground, the bottle out of sight now, "Let's go, they're just hanging out."

Varsity jacket runs his hands through his hair but when he does it he upsets his glasses and they almost fall off his face. He rests them on the hood of his car.

"If I hit you, you'll cry," he says kind of evenly. "Your son doesn't want to see that."

"For fuck's sakes…" I say and look at the girl.

He starts to walk towards my father slowly, casually, his hands at his sides.

And you know what? He was right.

On our last morning in the green hotel he woke me up in my Spiderman pajamas, the warm air pushing softly through the open curtains of the balcony that overlooked the beach. I could hear kids my age playing and they'd come into my dreams while I was sleeping and in my dreams we were all playing together.

"Hayden, wake up…I have something to show you."

Down to the lobby, out the double doors, down the white steps to where the moss was, the small palm trees. I was still half asleep, but I was waking up; all that life. The sun didn't look orange, it looked red, and very hot.

I walked behind him towards the far end of the property, him in his black t-shirt.

When we got to the little bridge he put his fingers to his lips and told me to stay where I was. Then he went ahead a couple of paces and, getting down on one knee to look underneath the bridge, he raised his hand up, motioning for me to come over.

It looked, at first, like a piece of wreckage...lifeless and old and rickety – but then it moved, its back rising up as it breathed.

"Have you ever seen something like that?" he asked me. He was amazed by it. I remember filing that away – the look on his face.

I was waiting for it to open its eyes.

"No, never."

"Me neither," he said.

We stared at it for a while. I thought about how fun it would be later to go swimming. Maybe after we got back to the house and had breakfast we could go swimming in the ocean. Or he could just watch me in the ocean. That'd be fine too.

"Is it going to open its eyes, Dad?"

Before he slams his forehead into the guy's chin, he leans back so far that his blazer rides up and I can see his pinstriped boxers and about a centimeter of his flesh. If he'd been taller, he would have killed him – he would have put his nose bone through his brain. The hit sounds like a vehicle exiting a wind tunnel but there isn't as much blood as I expect, a small shroud erupting from the guy's lip before he blacks out and falls over. The girl laughs out of shock, which is weird, and runs around the Acura to kneel next to him. She puts her hand under his head, her knuckles on the concrete, and looks at me with those snowstorm eyes.

He's running in front of me now, his blazer flapping in the wind. It looks like some vile television commercial about businessmen following their true passions. We run through alleyways, the sounds of the street entering and fading and entering again. There is music and we run towards it, instinctively. We stop, panting, in front of a vibrating metal door illuminated by a yellow security light.

I light a cigarette and stare at his bloodstained forehead.

"Bullies, man…bullies! Fuck I'm happy I did that!! Jesus I'm happy. Jesus fucking Christ I'm happy!!"

His voice drops into his throat and he hits a pretty damaging rasp when he says "happy" for the second time.

"I haven't done enough of that in my life," he says, exhaling, the yellow light on his feet.

The yellow light moves to his neck as he gets down on his knees, clasps his hands together, and closes his eyes.

"Thank you!" he yells. "Thank you!!!"

Two massive black transvestites come out the door talking like high school girls. I hear one of them say, "Like, she's soooo *extra*…" before they look at my father on his knees and keep going.

He keeps his eyes closed and says "I'm not apologizing, Hayden."

"Who is asking you to apologize?"

"I'm done apologizing, Hayden, you need to respect that."

"I do, Dad…I respect that. But check this out…I want you to listen to what I have to say. I realize this is a *difficult evening for you*…"

I can't get that one out without laughing. He opens his eyes and beams at me, grinning.

"You're a funny guy, Hayden."

My voice gets deep. It's like a different person saying it.

"You have to understand that you've *stolen* that place from me. It was my place, something for me, something I'd accomplished – and you've taken it. It is now just a place where you head-butted a guy. I was proud of that, and you've taken it."

He puts his knees to his chest and sits down in the alleyway. He looks up at me. He is really listening now.

"You take shit from me, you take things…" I say. "You know, when I die…"

"That's a long way away," he says.

"When I die, I want to look back and think about something other than you. Sometimes I can't tell the difference

between us. When I die I want to look back and see me…
so that's why I light the fires. That's why I do it."

His face is ghost white.

"This must look like war paint," he says, motioning to
the blood on his forehead.

"It is," I say.

"What is it you want, Hayden?"

It's a little bit like cliff-jumping – terrifying, all that
indifferent air. You look over the edge, your buddies going
"don't look over the edge, man, just jump…you're going to
trip yourself out."

One of them appears next to you, soaking wet, and says,
"Are you sick to your stomach? You have to go, it will ruin
your weekend if you don't…you'll be thinking about it all
fucking weekend, man."

And he's right, and so you wait until, there, you feel a
gap between seconds and then you jump, arms flailing away.

All the indifferent air beneath you.

"I want you to die," I say.

He gets up off the ground and walks towards me. For a
moment I think we're going to fight.

I'm too weak, though, too stripped from the dope and
the dreams and from him – too stripped from the white
stuff in Samantha's underwear.

Too weak.

That's not how warriors behave. I'm too weak.

He stops in front of me and I imagine the head butt.
Maybe it will kill me, I think.

Fine, I think.

Let's go underwater then.

I close my eyes.

I feel my toque being lifted from my head, and then I
feel his hands move through my hair.

"I know you do," he says. "And I don't blame you…you're
a nice guy, Hayden."

I let ten seconds pass before I speak. I keep my eyes
closed, my back straight.

"So you're going to do it?"

"Of course I'm going to do it…you think I want to wake up hung-over with blood on me? No, tomorrow morning is one that I am opting out of. It's okay that you want me to die… as long as you love me. You love me?"

I feel like I'm floating, with my eyes closed like that. The breeze on my face.

"So you're going to do it?"

"Yes, I'm going to do it. Do you love me?"

"Yes," I say.

"Then it's okay…"

He deposits my toque in my hand and I put it back on.

Two Native drunks, the kind with the skin you get from drinking gasoline, circle and weave around each other at the edge of the alley. They laugh until one of them falls over and they laugh harder. One helps two up and they continue.

We walk until we find a taxi at the very south of Parkdale, by the lake. The sky and the water look exactly the same, the stars and the white ripples exactly the same.

We get into the cab and my Dad gives him the directions to our house. I feel empty and kind of nice, like I've made love. I'm looking forward to a shot – I'm looking forward to calling it a day.

My phone goes off, it's Damon.

I'm in front of your place buddy I stashed my dope in your flower pot LOL.

I show my Dad the text and laugh. He half-laughs and looks out the window.

"You still have blood on your forehead," I say.

And it's strange, for a second he looks embarrassed. He looks ashamed. He wipes his forehead quickly, like a kid – as if the speed in which he cleans it will erase everything.

It's okay that you want me to die.

I repeat the words in my head as we drive by those white word advertisements etched into AstroTurf on the highway. They are lit up like little baseball fields.

It's okay that you want me to die.

A jazz song that sounds suspiciously like the one from the taxi before fades in. If it's the same it means it's all on a loop, that there is no DJ in some loft somewhere sharing his evening with us.

I scan the words until I distill what is wrong with them. I've always been good at that. We pull up onto our street and I can see Damon, his chin raised up, talking to our neighbour. He looks like a handsome gargoyle, half of his hair in afro, the other half in corn rows. He turns to face the taxi and you can see his small, angry freckles and his shark eyes. You can see his mouth – there's a lot of irony in that mouth. He has a lit cigarette in his hand and he's laughing at something the neighbour has said.

It's okay that you want me to die.

He's given me permission. He has, in his way, taken *that from me*, too.

I look him in the eye before I say it because movies have taught me that's what men do when they're telling the truth.

"If for some reason you don't do it, Dad. If for some reason you *do* wake up tomorrow morning…and this was all bullshit…"

And I am telling the truth when I say it.

"If for some reason it doesn't happen…*I'm going to do it.*"

The cab stops. Damon is wearing a long cargo jacket and he looks magnificent out there in the night. There are some people who really belong out there in the stars, under the water, and he is one of them.

"Did you hear what I said?"

He nods, hands the driver some money and gets out of the taxi. Damon throws his arms around him and kisses him on the cheek.

They've always liked each other.

"Keep the change," I say.

And then I hear it, the voice:

And tonight we have something very special…very, very special…I heard this as a young man and it came to me the other day so I thought I would share it with you all…

TWO A.M.

Damon has this habit of getting girls' phone numbers and then promptly sending them pictures of his penis. He's always trying to show me their text message reactions on his phone but he never scrolls down properly and I always end up seeing his dick. I've seen it like twenty-two times.

Tonight is no different. When my Dad goes into the house, and we're standing in front of the flower pot, he pulls his phone out of his jeans.

"Look what she said, check this out. ..."

"Scroll down properly."

"What do you mean?"

"I don't want to see your dick."

"Obviously, bro..."

He passes me the phone; a small pink word reads *nice*.

"Cool," I say.

"I don't think she would have said that if she didn't mean it, right?"

"How long did you wait to send her the picture?"

"I got her number yesterday."

"Do you ever think that you should wait a little bit?"

He considers that for a second.

"No."

I laugh and light a cigarette. I watch our neighbour go inside.

"What were you talking to him about?"

"The Raptors."

"I didn't even know he spoke English. ...Aren't you worried you're going to freak them out?

"The girls?"

"Yeah."

"Nah, it ain't about that."

"What's it about then?"

"It's about…I don't know…I like the way their face looks in my head when they see it. 'Cause they're not expecting it…you know?"

"Okay, I get that."

"Right? See, I know if anyone understands that shit, you understand it."

We robbed a house together when we were young, fourteen or so. He's a lot taller now. We did it well, both of us slowing down with every step, feeling the anxiety and accepting it. We didn't talk about it but we both know that was the way to do it…slow down…slow down.

We got robbed for the stuff after, some Jamaican in some park somewhere who Damon said he knew. He left with our knapsacks and never came back.

I always had a suspicion that Damon ended up getting his cut, but that was fine – it wasn't about the money for me. It was about the story. It was about the money for him, so that was all fine.

"You want to go inside?"

"Fuck, man, you freaked me out now about sending that shit. You always do that…"

"Do what?"

"Make me worry about shit…make me self-conscious."

"Really?"

"Yeah, man."

"I'm sorry Damon, that's shitty…I don't want to do that."

"So how long should I wait, then?"

"Why wait? It's about the surprise, like you said."

"Yeah, it is."

He scoops something out of the flower pot and places it in the breast pocket of his cargo jacket.

"You know who I *seen* tonight?" he says.

"Who'd ya see?"

He grins at me.

"Samantha…I saw Samantha tonight."

I want to go inside and get high now. I don't want to talk anymore.

"We should go inside. You want a drink?"

"I talked to her."

"Damon, I don't want to talk about Samantha."

"Why are you saying my name like that?"

I exhale and squat down on the porch the way you see the Asians do. They must have something in their legs, some elasticity to their muscles that allows them to crouch like that. I can only do it for a couple of minutes. I look over to the abandoned house. The sign is still lit up, but it will be out soon.

I stare down at the porch and the lines in the wood *start to move.*

Keep looking at the lines until they stop moving...

I hear Damon above me. "Hey, what's wrong with you?"

I hear his voice in one ear and then it kind of shifts through my brain to the other. I reach down for my cigarettes but my hands are shaking and it embarrasses me and so I stop and leave it at my sides. The lines are still moving.

I don't want to be here anymore. I want to be in bed with Samantha. I want to listen to the air conditioner in her room.

I close my eyes and I'm not surprised at all when they appear in the dark moving the same way.

With my eyes closed I take my right shoe off, and then my sock. The air feels nice on the cut.

"Does this look okay?" I ask him, motioning to my foot.

"Let's go inside."

The same stereo shift from one ear to the other.

"Here, let's go inside, Hayden. I got your dope. Do a shot, something..."

My legs crumble underneath me and my ass slams into the wood. I think about my ass hitting the lines.

"It's because I'm not Asian," I say and laugh.

"If you come inside I'll tell you what Samantha said about you...it was good, you'll like it."

"Okay," I say.

I open my eyes and he's standing above me. He looks legitimately concerned and of course that makes me want to burst into tears.

"Did you get the cut of money from that house…when we were little?"

He doesn't know what I'm talking about.

"The house we robbed!"

"Keep your voice down, man…"

The front door opens and my Dad comes out. His hair is wet, he's showered. He looks down at me.

"Come inside, Hayden."

"Did you take the money?"

"Of course not, brother – let's go inside…"

"You owe me money," I say.

I knew, as I soaked my foot in the tub, Damon and my father laughing and drinking martinis downstairs, that I needed to stay straight for the next couple of hours.

I've had sleep problems since I was fourteen years old, and ever since then, I could always pinpoint the shift in mood when the sky turned warm black *to that other colour.*

The dust on the floor, on the legs of my bed, on the door handle seemed to glimmer and say, "It doesn't matter how hard you work, something very bad is going to happen to you."

So you have a drink, you do a line, you get on the phone and try to get laid, you put your ninja turtles out on the living room floor and you *focus.*

I yell out, "Damon! Come up here! I want to show you something!"

I hear the murmurings of their conversation closing and then Damon's footsteps up the stairs. He knocks on the door and comes in, surveys me with my foot in the tub.

He says, "You really like to *unwind,* don't you, bro?" and laughs. "You want your pill now?"

"No," I say.

I want a cigarette but I've left them in my pants pocket.
"How's my Dad?"

"He's good – come down, man, join the party, bro."

"Will you go get my cigarettes for me? I want you to tell
me about Samantha."

I expect him to say no but he nods and says, "Where are
they?"

"In my room, next to my bed, in my pants."

"Okay," he says.

He's not used to drinking, especially drinking with
someone like my father, and he kind of wobbles when he
comes back into the bathroom with my smokes. He sits on
the edge of the tub, looks into it at my foot.

I take a cigarette from the package and put it at the
corner of my mouth.

"Fuck, I don't have a lighter."

He pats the breasts of his jacket, then gets up and
searches his jeans. He pulls out a gold Zippo and lights it
with two hands.

"Tell me about Samantha."

"She asked about you, that's all, bro."

"What'd she ask?"

"She asked how you were doing."

I gesture around me.

"Did you tell her?"

"No, I told her you were in law school."

"Fuck off."

"Yeah, funny right? She believed me, though…"

"Why didn't you tell her the truth?"

"What truth? This? Nah, man…that wouldn't be good."

I nod. The water on my foot is cold now.

"Did she say anything else?"

"She said she liked kissing you…she was drunk, I don't
know. She just said that shit, "I liked kissing him," and then
she went back off with her friends.

"What were her friends like?"

"Girls…"

"Right."

Damon has always been a little bit obsessive about my hygiene. Even before the drugs, it's always irritated him that I only showered a couple of times a week. He would never, for instance, slap hands with me if he had the feeling that I was unwashed…he'd put his knuckles out instead. When he did that we'd fight about it. He grew up very poor, so he was always fastidious about that stuff.

He dips his freckled hand into the tub.

"Here," he says.

He pulls the stopper out and drains the tinted water. Then he plugs it back up and runs it hot.

"When you're done, come down…I gots to go soon."

"You *gots to*, eh?"

"I *gots to*."

ა

Samantha had been gone for two years and there was blood on Damon's kitchen floor. I sat staring at a Wu-Tang Clan sticker on his refrigerator while he poked around on my arms and hands with the needle.

It seemed that my veins had retreated for the day – and I needed help.

I was doing Dilaudid at the time, I think, the tiny yellow footballs that dissolved in water – you didn't even need to cook them.

He had, at that point, disregarded his rule completely. Looking back, there were probably many reasons for it: he wanted to give me some relief, he liked my company, the monetary thing…

When he finally found a vein and fired it into me, he washed his hands aggressively in the kitchen sink and then stood in the middle of the room and told me he was depressed. I told him it was because he was a drug dealer, and being a drug dealer is depressing. Making a lot of money for doing nothing is depressing…very simple.

He nodded and smiled and agreed with me – he handed me a Lysol rag and told me to wipe the blood off the ground.

He said he saw my father in the newspaper. Then he asked me why I never called Samantha. Why I didn't just fucking call her?

I told him, stoned like that, the words meaningless and floating to the rafters as I spoke them, that she was only a human being – she was only a human being and she'd taken on *more important* work in my heart and I didn't want to disturb that.

I didn't want to know whether she still loved me, whether she thought about me.

I told him that sometimes I imagined her with other men. I imagined her fucking other men, I imagined her trying to please *me* through *their bodies*.

He took one of my cigarettes off the table and lit it – he wasn't a smoker so he held it kind of effeminately.

Yellow Skin was coming by in a little bit, he said. I had to go.

I went to an after-hours bar in Parkdale that night. I lost fifty dollars at the poker table and did a line of coke in the foggy one-bathroom stall with an acne scarred guy in a Nike hoodie. That's the after-hours experience, in a nutshell.

Around four o'clock in the morning the place got raided. There was something primordial about watching the blacked-out swat guys bust in through the smoke and the shiny-mouthed blonde girls in tank tops and fedoras at the entrance. I've seen it a couple of times, at first it almost seems like a joke – like someone showing up in a Halloween costume. But then you can feel the aggression, the movements of the cops so focused and strained compared to everyone else floating around like they do in those places.

They made everyone get on the ground – it was exciting, actually. The redhead next to me, with the pure white outfit and the twitchy jaw, grinned and said "shit" before she lowered herself onto the floor. She had a tattoo of a castle on her outer forearm, and I could smell her perfume while we were down there. She turned her head to look at me three times while the swat guys yelled at people and arrested the owner. It was like we were in bed together.

When I got home around five with stains on my clothes, the birds starting to chirp, my father was in his study painting. He'd started on some meds a couple of months prior and they seemed to be leveling him out a little bit. He'd always been concerned about going on antidepressants; he worried it would fuck up his painting.

It didn't – he'd made a sale a couple of months earlier that had paid off the mortgage on our loft.

I couldn't help but equate this shift with the evening I'd asked him to paint me, after I'd lit the fire in the field.

It was, looking back, my surrender to him – and while I degenerated, he thrived – it's just the way it was.

I'd stopped working completely and I was shooting about eighty dollars a day in pharmaceuticals (sometimes a little junk, too). This was a luxury I could afford with the occasional handout from my Dad and by working part-time for Damon – dropping off eight balls to dying house parties at three o'clock in the morning.

There were some nights, standing on a stranger's porch with cocaine stuffed into my boxers, that I swore I could hear her voice over the dim music, or see half her face, or half her teal sweater illuminated in the window. At first it scared me, made my chest tight, but as the months went by I started privately hoping it would be her to answer the door.

It never was.

Knock, Knock, Knock.

He came out of the study in clean pajamas, a coffee mug in his hand.

He told me that Damon had been calling, that he'd tried me on my cellphone.

He was in the hospital.

The first thing Damon said, lying on his side with his head in his hand, the turquoise hospital gown looking odd, almost demented on him, was: "Fucking guy tried to cut my dick off."

His right eye was completely swollen shut and his arm was in a sling, demolished.

There were deep cuts on his face and on the side of his neck and his nose was broken.

While he sold opiates and hash, Damon's main source of income was cocaine. Once a week, a rental car from Montreal would arrive at his King Street apartment (Sherbourne and Queen was long gone by now) and drop off four vacuum-sealed kilograms. He'd keep one brick for himself for smaller sales, and middle-man the rest. One of those bricks, every week, went to Yellow Skin – who, along with increasingly violent home invasions, had started to move up the ladder.

What Yellow Skin hadn't known, until that day, was that, at some point, Damon had started cutting the bricks with numbing agent and re-pressing them so they looked brand new. It was an uncharacteristically greedy move. To this day I'm not sure why he did it.

Maybe 'cause he was depressed?

About an hour after I'd left, Yellow Skin had showed up with a couple of Vietnamese guys. They were there for the weekly re-up. They'd asked him if he was re-pressing the bricks…

"A rhetorical question, bro…"

They beat him for a little while, sat him down on the couch, and, with a gun to his head, took his pants off.

Yellow Skin put a buck knife to him, and told him he wanted every brick, and every dollar bill in the house.

They got away with ten thousand dollars and two bricks.

They didn't get everything; of course, he kept the main stash in a wall safe of the apartment of a graphic designer named "Sophie" who lived in a basement in Rosedale.

She was a nice a girl, he paid her rent.

When visiting hours were over he told me to come sit next to him. He wasn't used to taking drugs, he was mostly a weed smoker, and so the painkillers had him slow, scratching himself.

"What's that shit, Hayden...it's like the word they use when people say shit all the time so it's not as good anymore because so many people have said it?"

"A cliché?"

"Yeah, a cliché... You know what the truth is? Money is more important than pussy...that's the truth...but that's a ...cliché, right? *Money over pussy*...Jesus, can you imagine if that fucking goof had cut my dick off? Bro, I feel blessed..."

Shortly after that, a month maybe, I rode the night bus to Parkdale with a duffel bag in my lap.

It was a Tuesday at four o'clock in the morning and the main street was empty except for a fat Somalian in a white hoodie, light blue jeans and worn lime green running shoes leaning against the all-night Shawarma place. The neon rainbow sign blinked above him, the purple being the most pronounced.

The after-hours looked a bit like someone's garage – a square bungalow at the beginning of an alleyway on Mortimer Street. I checked the windows for alarm stickers. There was nothing. I went to the back and counted to fifty, then I smashed the window with the dope-smashing hammer from my duffel bag. It barely made any noise; it sounded like someone might have dropped a beer bottle on the street. I did it so gently. It was impressive, actually.

I climbed through the window. The duffel bag caught, I went slack and tried it again.

The place felt especially sordid with no one in it. It smelled like sawdust.

I could see the aluminum bar with the mirrors behind it near the front entrance. The mirrors glinted in the black. Unlike the park, or the field, there was nothing here that reminded me of home. I considered that.

I spun the flask of lighter fluid slowly on the bar until it pointed where I wanted it to – to the purple couches directly behind me. I took the newspaper, a *Toronto Sun* sports section, and stuffed it into the cracks of the couch behind the cushions. I pushed the couches quietly to opposite walls and doused both of them with about half the can of fluid. I stood on the couch and stuck some of the paper I had left into the rafters.

Then I sprayed the floor.

The lighter fluid didn't smell like a dream, like I remembered in the field. It smelled very real – too real, like the dry mouthed sensation of coming to from a nightmare, hung over.

It smelled like five years in prison.

When I thought I heard a knock at the window I felt my bowels contract. I dry-heaved and ducked down behind the bar, forcing myself very still. I sat there in the dark, the fluid stinking more and more – I wondered for a moment if it was making me hallucinate.

No knocks after that.

I asked Damon once why he started selling drugs. He told me he was fourteen, living with his crazy mother in the east end. She'd gotten into the habit of calling the police on him for looking at her the wrong way.

"Threatening glances!" he'd hear her telling the cops over the phone.

He did great imitations of her. Another story was the time he'd thrown a meatball at her during dinner. It had hit her in the forehead.

She'd looked at the clock to note the time.

"Six thirty!" she'd cried out. "Six thirty! Assaulted! With a meatball! *By a criminal!*"

That was my favourite one.

One day he woke up, looked out the window, and said to himself: "I will never be broke again."

I sat behind the bar, getting sicker – my duffel bag beside me. I stood up and looked out the filthy tinted window. No shapes.

I took the ten books of matches out of my pocket. Everything went very cold for a second.

I kept the matches attached to the book and twisted them around to scrape them across the flint; they went up almost one at a time, and when they did I had a fireball in my palm. It watched it go. Stepping onto the couch, my feet sinking into the purple fat, I laid it softly in the ceiling. It sputtered for a second and then went, a lightning bolt of brown smoke shooting into my face. I stumbled off the couch and fell over. Without getting off the ground, the small flames like lantern sharks in the corner of my eye above me, I lit the second book and threw it at the purple couch pointed west. It landed where it needed to.

I didn't get the hit right away so I took my shirt off and threw it onto the flaming sofa. It went up like tissue paper. My arms, lit up by the lantern sharks, were fucked – absolutely hideous with tracks.

I stood in the room shirtless and watched the fire. Then it came. I stood there until I heard sirens. It struck me that I'd never lit a fire and heard sirens before.

It was different with Damon. That's the best way I can put it. I realized that day, looking across from him in the hospital, a bruise running from his foot to his abdomen so devastating it looked alien, that I'd known this guy since he was a kid.

I didn't know why it was like that, when our cells connected like that, why God put us together in Toronto for all those years…

But I felt, back then, that he was close to something ugly and final – and I loved him, and only I knew how much I loved him.

It was untouched by my father, or Samantha's phantom, or by the drugs…

It hit me that I'd attained something. Something that I, *Mr. Self-Aware* himself, hadn't even noticed until it had already been created.

And even though this untouchable thing, this beautiful calcified *thing* had been marked on its own, I wanted to mark it myself – before he went underwater.

℞

I get a dress shirt out of my closet – it was a Christmas gift from Samantha's mother, a grey button-up from the Gap that I've never worn. It feels nice to put on a clean shirt. It's always been too short, but it looks good in the mirror. I can see my unmade bed behind me in the reflection. I try not to look at my eyes.

What will law school be like?

FOUR A.M.

The party has moved from the living room to the back balcony. I watch them tip their martini glasses through the bay windows. Damon's grinning and wearing his hood, half of it puffed up from his hair. My Dad has his feet up on the white patio table – it's strewn with blunt ashes, two cans of beer, a fresh forty-pounder of vodka with a quarter of it missing. I get an orange pop out of the fridge and stand at the balcony doors sipping it and watching them. When they notice me they usher me outside.

My Dad gets up and says, "Here, take my chair, I'll get another chair."

"No, I'll stand, it's okay."

Damon looks up at me from under his hood. His smile is that of a confused infant. It's the expression of someone who is about to crash, someone who can't hold their liquor. My Dad and I don't make expressions like that. The straight vodka is killing him.

"Nice shirt," my Dad says. "I've never seen that shirt before."

I run my hand over the collar and nod.

"Damon was just telling me about all the drugs that he sells..."

Damon takes his hood down, reaches across the table and lays the oversized wrist of his cargo jacket gently across my father's forearm.

"You got to keep your voice down a little bit," he says, his face returning to the stupor as his arm extends back onto his lap.

He whispers, "Sorry, sorry," and puts his palms up flat.

Damon nods and closes his eyes, seemingly appeased by the volume change.

"What about Valium? You sell Valium? You know, I used to sell Valium in the early eighties."

"No, people don't like them," Damon says. "Valium is a bullshit drug, anyway…I think so, anyway."

"You sold Valium, Dad?"

"For a couple of summers, yeah – you know that's how Paul Newman's son died?"

"Who's Paul Newman?"

"You've never seen *The Hustler*?"

"What's that?"

"It's a pool movie…with that fat guy in it. Who's that fat guy, Dad??"

"Minnesota Fats."

"Right."

"And his son died from Valium?"

"Valium and beer."

"Oh wait, isn't he the one with his face on the tomato sauce?"

"No, that's the fat guy with glasses."

"No, he's on the tomato sauce thing, too."

"Yeah, I know that fucking guy. You know, when I was doing my last bid, they called Valium *War Pills*, bro."

"*War Pills*. Wow, that's a great name."

"Hayden, throw me my lighter. You'd do nine of those things if you knew you had to scrap – because they make you angry."

"No, they relax you."

"No, they don't…you just think they do. They make you angry."

"Damon, I've done them fifty two thousand fucking times. They relax you."

"Nope, they're *War Pills*, trust me."

"I can't find your lighter…I think it's in the bathroom."

"There are so many hot girls in Toronto, man – on the subway…you ever notice that? We have the most beautiful women in the world. How do you choose the one you're going to marry?"

"You choose the one you meet."

"What if you meet a lot of them?"

"You never meet a lot of them, you just think you do."

"So how long are you going away for?"

"A couple of months..."

"You're going to miss the winter...lucky fucking guy. Hayden, your Dad's a lucky fucking guy. How are you going to get the pills across the border, though?

"They don't check old guys like me. I'll just put them in one of my fifty prescription bottles."

I watch Damon's face as this lie tumbles out...he's sharp, Damon...and a good liar himself. He doesn't seem to notice, though.

He reaches into his breast pocket and takes out the pill bottle. The prescription sticker has been blacked out with a sharpie and he's stuffed it with gauze so it doesn't rattle. He places it soundlessly in the centre of the table and starts doing math in his head.

"Three-forty...you know what...no...Three-twenty is cool. Yeah, three-twenty."

"Sounds good," my Dad says.

He gets up and goes into the house. A plane passes above, followed by an argument in Chinese two blocks away. It's not a good sound – it makes the trees around us seem flimsy. It's only going to get worse, too. The world is coming in.

I reach over and pick the martini up.

The screen door slides open and a stack of creased twenty dollar bills scatter across the table.

"There's three-forty..."

I've seen Damon count money many times. He's careful with it. The face has to go in the same direction...two folds with a rubber band...

His eyes get small as he notes the disrespect of the currency.

"It's three-twenty..."

"It's fine. Three-forty is fine. Thank you, Damon."

He counts the money, and then counts it again. He pauses, his eyes flit to me, and then back down to the money. His posture seems to change while he's counting it, his back straightens.

"It's three-forty," my Dad says.

"No, I know, I know that…I'm just trying to figure something out. Just figure something out…just how much money I spent today…I'm just…"

There's nothing wrong with the money, and although he is trying to *figure out something*, it's not how much money he's spent that day. Something has entered him in the slim gap of time between the bills being thrown haphazardly on the table and the sound of the plane and *the war pills*.

He is an intuitive guy but he won't get it, I think.

I watch his eyes, I watch him replay the entire evening.

"Where did you say you were going again?" he says, his hands still shuffling unconvincingly with the bills.

"Paris," my Dad says.

"Right, Paris – nice. You know what? I'll have another drink with you guys…fuck it, my day is done anyway…"

My father, like a hex in the afternoon breeze, looks over at me and smiles. He keeps his eyes fixed on me. There's pride in his eyes, the way he looks at me. He likes the way I look.

He reaches out and puts his hand on Damon's shoulder.

"I'm tired, Damon. You have to go. …Another time."

Don't look sad, I think. You'll figure it out soon.

He looks at my Dad, and then back at me. He puts the money into his jacket and takes his hood off. He puts his face in his hands, and then lowers them – grinning sadly over his palms.

"Okay, then," he says and repeats it. "Okay, then."

He pulls his hood off and runs his left hand through his afro, and then pats down the corn rows on the other side. He stands and looks at me.

"I'll see you tomorrow, man," I say.

He nods and pats the twenty pockets on his cargo jacket, and looks at me again.

My father picks the pill bottle off the table and holds it in his right hand by his side. He leans against the patio entrance with his other arm.

When we're back inside, my father squints at the clock next to the photograph of me in front of our old apartment building. I have my skateboard and wrist guards on. He only made me wear a helmet for ramp stuff. Damon sits at the bottom of the staircase and starts to put on his Wallabees. My Dad stares at him impatiently for a second, and then he stops.

"Damon," I say. "You want to see a painting? You want to see a painting before you go?"

There are books on painting in the study, yes, but mostly the small wooden room is lined with books on war: *World War One, The Mexican Revolution, The Mongol Conquests.*

There are hundreds of them. They are the wallpaper.

The flooring is newspaper; my eyes scan something about taxes from 2003, something about Rosie O'Donnell, a father and son killed in an avalanche in Alberta, more shootings in neighbourhoods where the only interesting thing to happen in them are shootings.

Behind the easel, behind the painting, is a red felt chair. I've spent a lot of afternoons in that chair, even before he ever painted me. He liked company while he worked. He'd say, "Shit, I should be doing this alone. That's how the real guys do it...but it's more fun with you."

I'd think about that. What did the *real guys* look like? Who were they? Why did they want to be alone all the time? They came from a different stock, had different blood. The idea of them scared me – made me think, even at that age, eight or nine, that we were doing something wrong.

But then he'd say it. He'd duck out from behind his easel and say, "But fuck 'em if they can't take a joke, right, Hayden?"

Man, I loved that.

In one sentence my father could wipe out the rest of the planet. They would disappear under smoke and once they ceased taking up *warmth*, and the alleyways in Chinatown seemed to glint with promise, I knew he was God.

And not only was he God, but I was an equal.

A lesser equal, but an equal, and that is more than I can say for the others.

He takes the tarp and folds it while Damon looks at the painting. The tarp won't fold properly, but he tries his best to do it nicely.

"That's crazy good. I like the way you did the boat," Damon says.

"Hayden doesn't like it," my Dad says.

"I like it more this morning," I say.

ଔ

My Dad left a thousand dollars in an envelope outside my bedroom door. It was the morning of my twenty-fifth birthday and I'd decided to go to a baseball game.

I'd never been to one before, but I'd heard my grandfather had spent the last fifteen years of his life watching it on television. He was a solid guy, my grandfather. An angry guy, yeah, but solid. He was a butcher over in the west end of the city. I remember him winking at me across a table in a food court once. My Dad says we only met once when I was two, so it's pretty wild that I remember that.

Shortly after I burned down the after-hours he fell apart again – he'd gone completely off his meds, just like that, no taper, nothing. He came into my room and told me why he'd done it. He had a philosophical reason for it – it was probably pretty good – I don't know...I wasn't really listening.

About a month after that, I heard something shatter in the middle of the night. By the time I got downstairs he was lying on the couch, his arm gushing blood. He was reading *The Hobbit*. He'd read it to me many times when I was little – he did the voices and everything. He was holding it in the air so he wouldn't get any blood on it, his wounded limb dangling off the side of the couch, a brownish puddle growing on the hardwood floor.

Damon called me from the gym in the morning to wish me happy birthday. He told me baseball was boring, but he'd see me later on.

When I got down to the water and I could see the Sky Dome about a half a mile away, I shot up in a Tim Horton's bathroom. I missed the vein and my arm puffed up and I didn't get a rush or even much of a high but it felt like that was the way it was supposed to go that day so I didn't do another one. I looked in the mirror of the bathroom stall and wished myself a happy birthday.

Happy Birthday, Hayden.

It was a cheesy thing to do but I left the bathroom feeling kind of happy.

I bought a chocolate milk and sat by the window and watched the guys in suits with briefcases and fresh haircuts move briskly through the sunshine. It occurred to me I never did stuff like that – never just sat there and watched people. I was always rushing through everything. When I was finished I smoked a cigarette out front – more guys in suits. They smiled at me. They weren't shitty smiles, either. Maybe they looked at me and felt sorry for me, or maybe they were just being nice, I don't know.

I told the scalper with the mullet and the long arms and the cigarette in his mouth that I wanted a seat not too close and not too far back. I told him I didn't want it to look *too* real, but I didn't want to be too far away either.

Without hesitation he gave me my ticket.

When I got to my floor, I started across the circular walkway outlining the arena. About every twenty feet or so there were corridors leading in. I bought a hotdog and a coke. From where I was standing, about eight feet back from the little hallway, it looked like a dead drop into the bright, bright green. I could hear the excitement, unintelligible like television snow, and I watched a skinny child in a baseball hat run ahead of his chubby mother and disappear into the static. I thought about calling my father and inviting him but I didn't. By the time he got there everything would have been different.

I entered with my hotdog and my giant pop and I could feel it in my lungs, all those people.

The seats were plastic but comfortable and there was a giant screen above the little men on the field. It was scanning the crowd. I was terrified for a moment that it was going to land on me – and then it passed. I thought about that for a while, that my mind had gone to that. There was no way around it, that's where my mind had gone to. It made me sad but then the dope amped up a little bit and all of that was lost. A lot of the people felt like that, so what?

My row was empty except for an older guy wearing glasses and a *Steelworkers* jacket. He had long grey sideburns. He must have been seventy. He was probably a union rep, that's probably why he had the jacket.

He looked over and then looked over again. The second time it irritated me and I stared at him for five seconds while he smiled pleasantly and watched the warm-ups.

I tried to keep my eyes on the field, on the warm-ups, but they kept bouncing back up to the Jumbotron. I noticed that it seemed to only fall on pretty girls. Even when it would pan to a group of cheering kids with their thumbs up there'd be some knockout with a baseball hat applying her lip-gloss in the background.

Whoever it was that got paid to scan the crowd was having fun with it. Some young guy, bored out of his skull in a tiny office on the top level.

When my father had gotten back from the hospital, his arm bandaged, I'd ordered a pizza and took two chairs from the kitchen and placed them in front of the window in the living room. We ate in silence, and when the pizza was finished he got up and took his chair and put it where it had been before. I kept mine where it was, and in a way, I didn't move from that spot for six months.

Waiting.

The Steel Worker said baseball was a boring game, but a good game. You learn to appreciate how boring it is as you get older. He took his glasses off and cleaned them. He used a small brown rag. His hands were tanned, darker than the rest of his body.

He introduced himself. I asked him why he was sitting next to me. He looked a little distressed when I said that. I'd hurt his feelings and so I started back-pedalling. I told him it was fine, I was just curious. I told him that crazy people always tried to talk to me.

"That's probably because they can tell you'll be nice to them," he said.

One night, making a drop for Damon, three guys had tried to rob me in the stairwell of a high-rise. It was only a matter of time, I guess. One of them had a knife but I could tell they were soft. They were soft in the eyes.

I sprayed the three of them with bear mace and kicked the one who'd had the knife in the head.

The screen panned to the catcher with his mask on. He was talking to the pitcher. You could see he was smiling even underneath the mask. He reached out and put his hand on the pitcher's shoulder, said something, and the pitcher laughed.

Baseball players had cool bodies – they were like real guys. Flabby asses, slight double chins. I liked that. They seemed very masculine – the kind of masculine I was.

My Dad stayed in his room mostly, leaving only an hour a day to paint. He said it wasn't coming. He'd lost it, he was sure of it. When he said that, I nodded from my chair in the living room and resumed staring out the window, the smell of the bear mace still on my fingers.

The giant screen was a distraction and it was annoying me. It was a bad thing, the screen. It wouldn't go away, though. It would be here longer than everything else in the stadium.

I told Steel Worker that I was going to buy my girlfriend a baseball hat, that I'd always liked baseball hats on girls: the way their hair came out the sides. It was sexy.

Someone shot Yellow Skin in the face on the front steps of an apartment complex in Scarborough. I'd read it in the paper. I knew it was him because I knew his real name: it had a staggering amount of letters in it. I had no idea if Damon was involved. I never asked him – never even brought it up.

Steel Worker got up and came back with beers for both of us. Then he grinned and unzipped his jacket, taking out a brand new Jays hat with the sticker still on it. He told me to give it to my girlfriend and wished me a happy birthday. I thanked him and got up, told him I had to take a piss. I wasn't planning on coming back.

He pointed across the field towards the blur of humans as I passed him. There were thousands of them. I couldn't see an empty seat.

"Do you see all those people? Every time they *move*..." When he said *move* I could tell he was Italian. "Every time they *move*, molecules move too...they move out of the way. We forget that sometimes. We forget that they make a difference in things."

I nodded and stuck out my hand.

"You don't feel that way, do you, Hayden?"

"No, I don't," I said. "But thanks for the hat."

It was dusk outside, that blue-grey colour. I thought about walking home, but by the time I got to the main intersection it was too cold, and so I got in a taxi and told the driver to take me north to Samantha's. When the taxi slowed down in front of her place I sat there in the back, in the dark, for a while.

I had no idea if she even lived there anymore.

I told the driver I'd come to the wrong place – but before we drove away I lowered the window and tossed the baseball hat onto Grayson Street.

I felt something drawing me back home, back to my father. I had been waiting for something, and it was coming, and all that waiting would mean nothing if I didn't get home right now.

He wanted to show me the painting as soon as I walked in the door. I told him I had to go to the bathroom first. His face got kind of coarse when I said that. He'd had a narrative in his head of how things were going to go – I was going to the come in the house, and go and see the painting. Having to piss hadn't been factored in and he didn't like it.

When I got back downstairs he apologized for being impatient, then we went into his study and showed me the painting.

It was of me.

Not just me, there was a ship too – a grey ship. The one he'd talked about the night he'd left the vodka in the snow. The Samantha ship, the one I was waiting at the port for. I was facing it. I was leaned over a small wooden fence separating the dock from the water and you could only see the back of me. My shoulders were hunched and it almost looked like I was holding a cigarette. He'd taken the way I lean now and put it on my eight year old body.

It was all the same, apparently.

The sky was white and *nothing*, and the ship, at first glance, looked sullen and alien and scarred by war – like something that'd come out of the sea. You couldn't see who was steering it, but I knew it wasn't Samantha. It wasn't Samantha in there, that's not what it was about, this was about something else.

He knew what it was, and he'd taken it. He'd painted it before it came in real life and that meant it wasn't going to come. He'd intercepted it.

He'd intercepted my ship.

I started asking questions to make myself feel better. I felt sick.

I started asking these questions…

Each time I'd stop myself and look at the painting again.

I went back to my chair at the window. I heard the front door close behind me. He was gone – probably out for dinner.

I stared out the window for what seemed like hours, my eyes on the abandoned house.

What is the sky?
The sky is over the planet?
What is the sky?
The sky is over the planet.
What is the planet?
The planet is something in the universe.
What is the universe?
The universe is black.
What is black?
Black is a colour.
What's a colour?

And so on.

Conversations between two dying versions of myself – both have chapped lips and lung cancer. The sign over the abandoned house was very bright and very beautiful. I have always loved Chinatown at night.

I stood in the empty living room of the abandoned house, a black plastic bag resting on the floor beside me. North was a doorway that led into the old kitchen. I could see a sink half ripped out of the wall and above it a window that looked across the street to our place. It was one of those old ones with a cross in the middle separating the view into four.

On the wall next to me there was a stripped and faded poster of an angel-faced blond child and a Chihuahua, both wearing bowties. It made me feel better that the people who had lived here were creepy assholes.

It irritated me that I was so nervous, though. This was, after all, the end. I was going to get caught for this one... there was no way around it, and it didn't seem fair that I had to be nervous at the end of everything.

I took the lighter fluid out of the plastic bag and went to the very back of the living room. I put my right foot next to the baseboard where the walls met and took the stopper out of the flask and let it pour as I walked forward to the opposite wall, then backwards and right, then back to the bottom of the room, and up again, until I'd made a giant 'H'.

He brought it up a couple of times when I was a kid, mostly while drinking, and always with good humour – these were not dark conversations, I must stress that. They seemed kind of bright and mysterious when I was that age.

He called it *leaving the party*.

Sometimes you've got to leave the party, Hayden.

And of course, because I was the age I was, I would picture something out of the nineteen-twenties: women in pretty gold masks and granite-jawed men in top hats. Sometimes I'd try to picture myself there, too. I never could.

I checked my phone; I hadn't heard from Damon all day.

I knelt at the edge of my giant 'H', and took the little box of matches out of my pocket. They were wooden firebirds that I'd found in the kitchen before I'd left.

As I knelt, I got an image of myself smoking a cigarette on the porch of the abandoned house, the yellow sign above me. I liked the way I looked – I looked handsome, shadowy, like a movie star.

When I look back on that moment, the redbirds in my hand, five seconds away from making one mark too many, a faded noir poster flashing behind my eyes, it was as if my brain was making one last effort at intuition, one last effort to save me.

My poor old brain, so shot out from the dope and the waiting that that's the best it could come up with.

Like a movie star.

Jesus.

I stashed the lighter fluid under the sink cabinet before I went outside to smoke.

The moon was a tiny sliver and there were no stars but it was warm, like day-heat almost. A Chinese woman in a winter jacket passed me with a shopping cart – she was our bottle collector. My Dad always made sure to give her the empties. We'd hear the clanking of her buggy and go out onto the porch to wave her up.

Those little insects were buzzing. I can't remember what they're called, but they buzz just like crickets except in my neighbourhood they're something different.

My house looked empty and still. He was still out for dinner. He wouldn't be home for a while.

A white Crown Victoria passed me and stopped about a block away. The dashboard was lit up. It looked like a console in a recording studio.

I heard my phone beep. A text from Damon.

I forgot nigga did I wish you happy birthday nigga? If I didn't…happy birthday nigga.

I put my phone back in my pocket and lit a cigarette, trying to look as casual as possible. The cop reversed and pulled up in front of me. I waved at him. He had curly hair, like a brillo pad – when he got out I saw that he had an ugly face but a strong body – swimmer's shoulders.

When he was in front of me he slapped the cigarette out of my hand.

"Easy," I said.

He slapped me in the face and threw me down on the front porch of the house – put his knee in my back, the whole deal. I let my body go completely slack while he cuffed me.

I didn't say anything to him in the back of the car. I didn't make up a story. I knew the stuff was under the sink but even if he found it he had no way of knowing anything, or proving anything. Even if he could smell the lighter fluid on my shoes, even if he went in there and smelled it on the floor, there was nothing he could say – no way to connect it.

No, as far as he knew I was just fucking around in an abandoned house. I didn't even say that, though, I just looked out the window and tried to think about something else.

As Damon used to tell me, "The more you talk, the better the chances you're going to jail, bro."

I was charged with criminal mischief and break and enter. He even tacked on resisting arrest but we both knew that was bullshit. I spent three days in jail. There's not much to talk about. There are no women there and therefore it is a *dead place*. Sometimes the violence and the nervousness around the violence can give off the same perfume as a girl walking into a party at night – but they are not the same, it is just an illusion.

On the third day I caught bail and met my Dad in the parking lot of the Don Jail. I was dope sick by this point, the withdrawal had started up – that agonizing restlessness in the legs, each moment a blurry, violent photograph.

He had a box of donuts for me and he was wearing a wrinkled white dress shirt and slacks with beat-up brown loafers.

I took a bite of the donut and spat it into the street.

Then I told him I couldn't see him anymore.

"Like ever?"

"I don't know…but not for a long time."

I didn't feel the need to look him in the eye. I didn't need to prove anything – all of that was over.

He put his hands on his hips and turned his back to me.

"I feel like I'm breaking up with a girl or something."

I told him I didn't know what to say. It was what it was.

In the cab he told me I didn't need to move out – that he was going to leave the party anyway – and did I mind calling Damon for him? And keeping him company?

When I got home I straightened myself out. I left the dope-smashing hammer next to my bed and the next morning I cut my foot on it.

Five A.M.

When Damon is gone I sit down in the red chair. My Dad looks out the window behind me and says, "This is not how I wanted it to go…I hate the daylight…I don't want to go out in the daylight."

"We've still got a couple of hours," I say.

He sits down on the newspaper floor below me and crosses his legs.

"Why thirty-four pills?" I ask him.

He puts his chin in his hands and says, "That's how old Jesus was when he died…a little *grand*, right?"

I laugh, he laughs.

"You want another drink?"

"No," he says.

"Well what do you want to do?"

"Talk…"

"Do you want to be alone?"

"Are you out of your fucking mind?"

"I just wanted to give you the option…you might be getting sick of me."

He takes his hands off his chin and rests his palms on the newspaper.

"I've never gotten sick of you, Hayden. Not for one second, not ever, since you were born."

"That's a nice thing to say."

We are in murky territory, here. I am getting sentimental. And I can see just past the clearing that there is a possibility I might start talking him out of it.

The more you talk, the better the chances you're going to jail, bro.

He looks out the window again. It really is ugly out there – it's still dark but in the fibers there is the threat of day. It probably wouldn't be as ugly if we weren't getting fucked up all night, if we had slept – but we have been, and we haven't.

I get up and pull the blinds over the window.

"I wish these were soundproof," I say.

"Me too," he says. "I want you to hug me," he says.

It is disgraceful but a strategic map flashes across my brain and I hesitate for a moment. Will it change anything? I bat it away and get down on my knees and put my arms around him.

I hold him for a little bit. He smells good. He smells like my Dad.

When we break apart his eyes are watery.

"I don't want to be melodramatic," he says. "But I can't help but think this is the last time we're going to hang out."

Not the last bit of night, not the last drink, not the last time he's going to be in his study, not the last time he's going to breathe...but the last time we're going to hang out.

"You don't have to use that preface," I say. "Be how you want," I say.

"What do you think is going to change when I'm gone?"

"Dad..."

"That's not an *adversarial* question, Hayden. I actually want to know. I'm curious."

"I don't know..."

He stands up and wipes his eyes.

"Yeah you do, tell me."

"You know I'm going to off myself if you don't, Dad – you know that, right?"

"That's what you said."

"But do you believe me?"

"I don't know...no, I don't."

He takes the pills and scatters them across the newspaper. He takes one and tries to break it in half.

"You can't break those in half, Dad."

"Jesus died when he was thirty three and a half...so I was going to give you the other half."

"You can't break them in half. ...I think, I guess, when you're gone, that I'm going to move forward. That's all. I am stuck. I am stuck somewhere because of you – and I don't blame you for it. I'm surprised more sons haven't *noticed this...*"

"More sons?" he says.

"More sons...I'm surprised more sons haven't noticed this."

"*Noticed this...*," he repeats. "You're a cool guy, Hayden. I like the way you talk."

He repeats it again... "Noticed this...hmmm, man... hmm...I'm going to have another drink. What time is it?"

We go into the kitchen and he fires up another round of martinis.

Move with it, I think, relax into it, like when you robbed the house. Slow down with it.

"You don't hate me?"

"I don't hate you, not at all – not for a second."

"You know you're going to have to push me down... when I fall asleep? The pills in themselves, that's not going to do it. I'm too fucking wiry."

He pours the two drinks and sets mine in front of me. We move back into the study.

"You almost put Damon in the graveyard with your martinis," I say.

He laughs.

"He's going to come to a bad end. He's a nice guy – but he won't end up like you..."

"You don't think I'm going to come to a bad end?"

"No, not at all."

"What do you think is going to happen to me?"

He takes a pull of his martini and says, "Well...I think you're going to have children. You must have children, Hayden."

"Why?"

"Because you need something to love outside of yourself."

"You're right, I guess."

"Women always let you down."

And he was right, they did – they always did, in the end.

"They don't mean to, I don't think – but they always do. If I've learned anything, that's what I've learned. That you must have children, and that women let you down."

"I don't think I can push you down," I say.

"Well how else will I go underwater?" he says.

"I don't know. Do you mind if I have a cigarette in here?"

"Of course not."

An hour passes, we fall in and out of sleep together. There are times I wake up and he's staring at me, times he wakes up and I'm staring at him. Each time this happens we resume the conversation.

He's in the middle of telling me a story about my mother, a nice one, when he stops mid-sentence. I know why he stops. The sky, through the blinds, has turned that blue-grey colour behind me. A part of me knew it was coming; it was the third member of the conversation that afternoon and I could feel its presence approach about half an hour before it did. I hoped he wouldn't notice, though. His voice, the way he speaks, the way he tells a story, has always hypnotized me.

"Well, look at that," he says.

"What?"

"I'm ready now."

"You want to go upstairs?"

"I do."

"You want another drink?"

"Nope."

"You sure?"

"Yup."

I take him by the hand and we exit the study and start up the stairs. Every stair he hits I look at as ten years, and by the time we're at the top he is two hundred years old. He takes his shoes off at the top of the stairs. I take mine off, too.

"My feet stink, I'm really sorry."

"All good, Hayden. All good…"

"Hold on – can you hold a second? I want to clean the bathtub for you. I cut my foot a while ago and I had my foot in it just a while ago and I'd like to clean it for you…"

"What happened to your foot?"

"I cut it, that's all."

"Okay," he says and we go into the bathroom.

He puts the toilet down and sits on it and I take the cleaning stuff out from under the sink and I run the tap lukewarm so I won't use up all the hot water. I use, for the first time in my life, an appropriate amount – I don't want to the bathtub to smell like chemicals.

I look over to him every couple of minutes to make sure he hasn't fallen asleep. The third time his eyes are closed and I tap him gently on the knee with my dry hand.

"Dad," I say.

"Yes," he says. "I'm still here, don't worry Hayden."

I always rush through everything but I don't with the bathtub. I do it by square inches, I make sure it's clean – I pretend I clean bathtubs for a living and if I don't do it properly I will be fired and my house will be taken away. Outside, *it* is at the centre of the blue-grey, the end period where the colours are thick and sturdy and about forty-five from fading completely.

"What are you going to do tomorrow?" he asks me.

"Be very fucking sad," I say.

When he's in the tub and the water's running I hand him the pills. I get him a glass of water. He takes three at a time until they are gone.

The buzzing from those *things* is very loud now. I think about asking him what they're called but he's staring off at the ceiling and thinking about something else.

"You never got any tattoos?" I ask him, looking at his small, toned body. I shut the water off when it's a little bit above his shoulders. He grins as if coming out of a nice thought and looks at me.

"No," he says. "What about you? I'm surprised you never did."

"Yeah, I don't know...," I say.

He nods and kicks his foot softly in the water.

"I'd like a drink now."

"Wine or martini?"

"Wine, a small one...you don't need to put it in a wine glass or anything..."

When I come back up with the small glass two inches filled with wine his eyes are red and half closed. I hand it to him. He takes a sip and holds it above the water so the bottom is almost floating.

"You know what I like about drugs?" he says. "About downers, anyway...you get this feeling...you get this feeling that you've *worked very hard*. You've worked hard, done well, but now it is time to rest...everyone deserves a rest from time to time..."

He puts the glass on the side of the tub with a clink and says "*How glorious that it is happening now, though?* I love you, Hayden."

When he closes his eyes, and they are closed for a while, the tub filled to his chin, I leave his side and move into the hallway and then into his bedroom. I lie down on his bed and think about how he'd wanted me to push him underwater, push him down.

My body starts to close and then I hear splashing and I am awake. There are snatches of voice in that limbo period between the two – this is not a new phenomenon – but they are louder than ever, they vibrate through me.

"I love these parties. It's too bad that you have to hit the fucking guy...but you do, so make sure you hit him hard, bro. Hit him hard – you don't want him getting back up, bro. *Shit, man, you don't want that...*"

"Night, Mom."

I bolt upright and look at the clock – only ten minutes have passed, it blinks eight A.M. It said all kinds of things while I was moving underground, which means I probably *was sleeping.* I take my button-up off and lay it across the back of a wooden chair next to the window that overlooks the alleyway behind the abandoned house. I watch the empty strip.

I have grown up in alleyways. I look at alleyways the same way kids from the suburbs look at the forest, or kids from the desert look at the sky.

I take a black t-shirt out of his closet and put it on. It's too small for me but it's alright. I make my way back down the stairs, passing the bathroom as if it doesn't exist.

I step outside and off my porch and into the street. It feels like a foreign country out there, like walking across the property of the green hotel all those years ago, the swimming pool illuminated and palm trees moving softly beneath the sun.

Samantha's shoes are still on the porch of the abandoned house. I'm surprised. Things don't usually go like that in Chinatown. The door is still ajar. It still smells like lighter fluid. I scrape the ugly poster off the wall with my house keys and find a spot on the ground and sit down so I can see the window and watch our loft.

It feels like a long time since I've slept, and so I doze off quickly, the buzzing from those little things still going and my father's words in my head:

How glorious that it is happening now, though?

Ten A.M.

I wake up to the sound of someone dragging a boot across the pavement, like they're trying to make a path of concrete through fall leaves.

The feeling is unmistakable.

My shoulders have broadened – the muscles have thickened, I know this because I can feel them pulling me up out of sleep and off the ground and placing me upright, at attention.

The clearness is scary. If I have gone insane, it's not bad – not bad at all. I think to myself, I must not be remembering correctly. Wait to remember, the bottom will fall out...and when it does, when you do remember what has happened, it's going to kill you.

It is a whisper in a different language. It doesn't feel like my language anymore but I placate it anyway on the off chance that it has to do with this new strength, this widening of the back, this new way I stand – I don't want it to go away.

I move across the wooden floorboards of the abandoned house and open the sink cupboard. The plastic bag is still where I left it.

I resume as if nothing has happened – I spray the ceiling, pause and spray the floor – back and forth, back and forth until the metal is empty. When I throw the flask in the corner where the walls meet and it clanks to the ground, it registers that I don't have a lighter– that I had to ask Damon for his fucking Zippo. There's a package of red birds across the way in our kitchen. It will take me less than a minute to get them.

Back outside the buzzing has stopped. It is silent and Samantha's shoes are gone. The morning light slants violently off rows of empty porches – harsh, tropical almost.

There is a figure in a navy blue hoodie standing lazily in front of our loft, boots planted in the cement, gazing up at the bathroom window.

Just the navy blue figure in the middle of the street and the little yellow window light above him – everything else in a coma.

He turns around as I approach and then looks back up without speaking. I place my hand on his shoulder and ask to borrow his lighter. He hands me his Zippo and I light one.

"You see the bottle lady?" I ask him. "Chinese, long jacket, even in the summer…takes people's empties…she hasn't come yet?"

He shakes his head.

"I'm surprised you haven't seen her yet…what are you doing?"

He takes his hood off. He looks pale, like he hasn't slept since I've seen him. The cigarette is lovely, just lovely.

He raises a baggy arm and points up at the window.

"I knew it. You want to know how I knew it?"

"How'd you know it, Damon?"

He puts his hand out and I pass him the cigarette. He keeps his eyes on the window as he speaks, as if something will be deciphered if he doesn't blink.

"So I get home, right? I knew there was something off with you guys, with the pills…*I just* knew…so I get home and I fall asleep and I have this fuckin' dream about your old man…and in the dream he's working for some magazine or some shit, right? And he's going to interview all these *rappers*…and we're chilling, getting high, and he's telling me about it. And I'm thinking, 'how the fuck is this guy going to interview a rapper'? But the more we talk, the more he tells me…and I start to believe him…then I woke up, and I just knew. "

I survey the empty street. No neighbour, no police officer, no one. I can't tell if Damon's angry, or in shock, or just Damon.

"You mad?"

"Nah, bro, I'm not mad…you got me caught up in some shit…but I'm not mad. You okay?"

He passes the cigarette back and drags a heel across the pavement.

"I don't know why I came back, bro. I don't think I would have tried to change anything…it's none of my fucking business, anyway. And *you know me*, right Hayden? You know *I mind my own business*…that's why I've survived as long as I have…anyway, your door was open so I went in…"

He pauses and his jaw tenses up, he spits through his teeth.

"Have you been in there, bro?"

"Not since…no."

He nods softly and pulls his hood back up.

"Okay…don't go in there…"

"I wasn't planning on it…"

He reaches out and he puts his hand on my chest, right above my heart – just for a second…then puts it back at his side.

"I have this feeling you think it's cozy up there…that it looks cozy…but it doesn't. You know? It doesn't look cozy. It doesn't look good…you got an image in your head of the way it looks…so keep it to that…that's good enough."

She's probably one of my first memories of the neighbourhood – first memories of life maybe. She wore a different coat back then…it was a different colour. I remember being thirteen or fourteen and waking up very early and going downstairs and seeing my Dad out on the porch waiting for her. He thought it was important to give her the empties. She'd come around once a week. As I got older, and we started to stay up late, we'd wait for her together. She was younger then.

"What did your Dad do, Damon?

"He was an inscriber…he inscribed shit…like gold… that kind of thing…that's what I hear, anyway…"

"It's good that you never had a Dad…that he wasn't around…"

"You think?" he says.

"Yeah," I say.

She wouldn't have taken Samantha's shoes. But perhaps one of her friends did? I imagine they all know each other – all the creatures.

"When you have a Dad, you're always trying to *mark things*, right? *Mark them as your own* – but you can't…you're always lagging behind…so you start setting these fires… you light the fires so you can say, 'I've been here…it was me…it was *me who did this…*'

I put my knuckles towards the concrete and I snap. I snap so precisely a small spark has been added to the painting of two tiny figures staring up at a yellow window.

"…and *bang*…just like that…you create your own planet. It's smaller than his, darker than his, his is always off to the right – it's always brighter than yours. So you spend your whole life lighting fires on your planet…trying to get it brighter, or at least, at the very least, the same. But it keeps *fading*…and so you have to light another, and another…gotta keep it going, right?"

Damon smiles slyly and puts his hood back up.

"Always gotta keep it going, bro…"

"Always," I say.

"And one day you wake up and you lie there with your eyes closed and you can tell before you even open them that he is dead. You are used to this *buzzing* first thing in the morning, right? It's all you know: this buzzing and this brightness that comes through even when your eyes are closed. So you know that morning, you know even before you open them that he is gone. His planet has vanished and you understand for the first time why you could never make yours like his – how the light was always different… no matter how many fires you lit…no matter how hard you tried…"

I hand him his lighter and then she's in front of our place. She's pushing a bundle buggy lined with red plaid. Who are her children? How long has she been doing this for? She looks over for permission. I nod and wave. She smiles and then opens the bin. There are more bottles in the house but I don't want to go inside.

She's known me for a long time – since I was a boy.

"To be honest with you bro, to be honest…I always kind of wished he was my Dad."

"Really?"

"Yeah, yeah, man…he was a solid guy. Regardless of the bullshit…he was solid."

"Yeah, all that," I say. "All of that…"

And when he gives me the signal, when he takes his hand off my face, when I say, "Okay Dad, I'm ready," we jump from the cliffs and we go underwater together.

There is a faint flickering down at the very bottom. Someone has built a little fire at the bottom and that is the destination. That is where we are going.

"Do you think we're going to make it?" he asks.

"Let's try."

"You got balls, Hayden. You got balls, just like me."

And even underwater I like that. Even in the dream I like that. I can feel my awake-body liking that.

And so we swim, past the white specks in the water and the police officers and the silence and we don't say much and we are very, very happy.

We're headed somewhere, me and him.

I'm swimming quickly and I can feel the pressure in my brain but I keep going, checking every once in a while to make sure he's still beside me. He is.

The little fire at the bottom of the ocean is getting closer now and I can feel the heat on my face.

"Can you feel that, Dad?"

He doesn't say anything, he's too focused on swimming – he's getting old, after all.

And it really is beautiful down there, once we are down there. He swims towards it and puts his hands out to warm them. It is something an older man does. Me, I just want to watch it go…

He says, "Do you see what I mean now, Hayden? Do you now know what I'm talking about? Isn't that something?"

And in the dreams I am the lesser God, the little God.

And that's okay.

In the end that's okay.

That's all okay as long as I am recognized as a God, too.

ACKNOWLEDGEMENTS

This book would not have been possible without the mind-blowing support of my agent, Sam Hiyate, and editor, Luciano Iacobelli. I cannot express how grateful I am to both of you.

I would also like to thank everyone at Quattro for their roles in the publication of this novel.

The following people have provided me with warmth and direction over the past two years: Thomas Hayes, Michael Amatulli, Vishal Bhandari, Maggie Keats, Conrad Lai, Victor Hayes Anne Mackenzie, Matt Scheulderman, Colleen Murphy, Maggie Gilmour, Jude Foster, Ebony Jansen, Jules Lewis, Iris Turcott, and Jay Szepesi.

Finally, I would like to thank my parents, Maggie Huculak and David Gilmour, for their continued faith, amongst many, many other things.